AF615183

"NONE SHALL HEAR YOU!"

The chilling words of the crippled seer hung heavily upon Rolind's troubled soul. Adrift on the ocean of perpetual storms where even the sea-warrior Bintus sailed with great concern, did Rolind search for the enchanted flower that would free him from his accursed Li.

Yet did he press onward, more fearful of those who would not listen—his own father and brother among them—than the death that waited beyond every crashing wave of the sea, every swirling gust of the wind, every piercing look of the ship's crew.

And then the flower lay upon his brother's chest. . . .

AVON
PUBLISHERS OF BARD, CAMELOT AND DISCUS BOOKS

ROLIND OF MERU is an original publication of Avon Books. This work has never before appeared in book form.

AVON BOOKS
A division of
The Hearst Corporation
959 Eighth Avenue
New York, New York 10019

Copyright © 1977 by Peter Lyle
Published by arrangement with the author.
Library of Congress Catalog Card Number: 77-77880
ISBN: 0-380-00981-1

All rights reserved, which includes the right to reproduce this book or portions thereof in any form whatsoever. For information address Avon Books.

First Avon Printing, July, 1977

AVON TRADEMARK REG. U.S. PAT. OFF. AND IN OTHER COUNTRIES, MARCA REGISTRADA, HECHO EN U.S.A.

Printed in the U.S.A.

To Dennis
R.I.P.

ODE TO ROLIND

What are you child

if not a creature of games, donning uniforms and disguises
seeking out the complexity of life
searching out a peace within the universe
and contentment with your mind?

What are you child

if not the lessons of your trials
if not the dreams which stimulate your mind
if not a personality begging expression in a reality so undefined
if not one tiny speck amongst the countless elements within the universe
if not a creature crying out in desperation, begging me who cannot read your thoughts or sense your fears to understand?

Does it take each generation of man

the murder of his kin
to make him understand
every man's relationship to him?

Or shall there be a way

to plant this lesson in the grave
and blossom for our children
a flower for their day, a flower
that will radiate the song,
to teach the way?

Are these abdurations in the night

which create the consciousness and light
to awaken mankind from the plight
of nature's wary flight

from those decades
when the human was a creature in the mud
and such a need
meant survival of the seed?

And shall there ever come a day

when the pain of life shall wane
and with our consciousness ablaze
understand that life is just a game devoid of rules?

But if it be the plan

to keep your nature as a man
won't you turn and face the grave
and rally with the knowledge
that one day
your suffering shall fly amongst the particles of
time.

Who are you child

if not the jewel of my eye
if not the questioning of mind
if not the answer to my universal, why?

if not my search throughout eternal time,
who I reach out to with this peace of mine?

And what be I

if not a child

once upon a time?

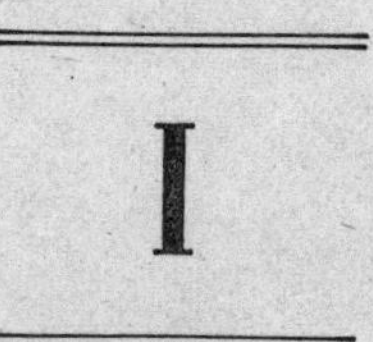

I

i

"You cheat!" shouted the fifteen-year-old to his twin. "Have you no respect for me?"

Prince Rolind of Meru arose, awed by the thought that Dels had discovered his ploy, and stared blankly at the foot-high pieces, trying to suppress a confession. The black jackal and panther blocked the ruby parrot and lead his brother to an assured victory. Rolind slowly raised his eyes from the green and brown continuum of diamonds and denied the allegation.

"You won fairly, I swear it."

"As I have won all our games this week," Dels protested. "By default."

"Dear Dels, you have too little confidence in yourself."

"Or perhaps it is you who have so little confidence in me."

The youth suppressed a tear.

Three oblique columns of morning light illuminated the small royal game room, shimmering off the red velvet walls and Rolind's orange silk shirt. His eyes remained in shadow, surveying the long shelves of books and games along the opposite wall, recalling how he had forfeited each day's play. And he carefully avoided Dels's hard stare, kneeling down, quietly clearing the checkered game cloth, hoping that his twin might not interfere any further with his plan. But as he touched a piece, Dels's hand slammed down, erasing all illusions of peace.

"Stop! You cannot surrender victory and expect me to accept it!"

"But it is I who lost."

"Only in appearance."

"Please, Dels. Don't accuse me in this manner. You won fairly, I swear."

"No I didn't! And I do not appreciate your deception. And although I understand the reason behind your strategy—seeing me win some mystical duel in the future—you cause concern where none exists!"

"Your accusation is not out of love!" Rolind angrily protested, rising up from the marble floor.

"Love?" Dels rose to face his brother. "You expect me to accept your words when I find you daily label love deceit?"

Rolind turned from his brother's anger, staring into a cloudless sky, watching seagulls circle effortlessly upon invisible paths. Oh, how he wished that Dels had never found him out. Oh, how he wished that Dels hadn't plucked away his only chance for peace. How easy it seemed, avoiding confrontations with reality; let Dels win, *although he loses every challenge in my dreams*! But no longer could he lie, and bowing humbly, Rolind answered with the truth.

"You are wrong, Dels. What you label deceit is fear. And through my actions I seek absolution of that fear. Besides, how can you question my love? Your eyes are as black as mine and these cheeks of yours, so narrow and indented are also *my* features. When I look into your face I see myself, and when I hear your voice, it is mine."

"But is it fair to see me dreading your personal fears?"

"They are not personal!"

"You should listen to *my* ideas and learn to recognize our differences instead of merely hearing my voice."

"You cannot deny our written fate!"

But Dels quietly knelt down, turning away from Rolind, and began gathering the tall carved figures, his voice calm across the room.

"What is written is not fate, merely history."

Rolind shouted, demanding his brother's attention. "You deny the evidence around us!"

"And you," Dels shouted back, "concern yourself with uncertainties!"

Rolind's eyes opened wide, not believing that Dels could say such a thing. Slowly he squatted down to stare into his brother's eyes, searching the face before him, hoping to find some sign of a lie; and when he could see nothing more than the reflection of his own eyes, he staunchly declared, "There *is* death in our future and I certainly do fear it."

"The only fear, my brother, is in your mind. The story to which you refer has no concern for us. Perhaps it *is* true that our ancient cousins made battle for the throne, but there exists no reason for us to repeat it," and he looked away.

"But the daggers lie within the castle walls . . ."

"And if they were hidden away, would it diminish your fears?"

"I would still sense their existence."

"And tell me, brother, which end of the dagger do you really fear?"

Rolind raised his head abruptly, not believing the words which his brother had just spoken.

"If you speak those words with humor, dear Dels, then I cry."

"Or are they merely dreams which frighten you at night?" Dels challenged.

"Oh, how I wish they were dreams!"

"Then tell yourself they are!"

Rolind raised an accusing finger at his brother and peered deeply into his eyes. "First you chastise me for deception in a game, then dare ask me to accept lies. That very idea proves your own hypocrisy and your fear in admitting what is obvious to all."

Rolind noted a tear which Dels couldn't suppress. A silence separated them, then Rolind stood.

"I have no wish to be king! Nor do I wish my own dear brother dead. But it is not by lies that we will change our pending doom. It can only be done by plan."

Dels turned away.

"You must relieve me of these fears," Rolind pleaded. "Whether they be real or simply demons in my mind!"

Dels continued his distant stare, but Rolind refused to permit his brother to avoid the confrontation.

"Simply tell *Father* that we have chosen. Here," Rolind said, clumsily exposing three pebbles from his pocket. "I have no wish to be king! I refuse! Here, draw one! Draw the white pebble! I want no part of this madness." He pushed the odd stone into Dels' hand.

"There," Rolind sighed. "Now you are the one. Now you are the next king of Meru."

"No!" Dels shook his head, denying the meaning of his brother's trick. "You play all games alike, dear Rolind. But you cannot win by deceit. Remember your own words —it can only be done by plan," and he shoved the pebble back into his brother's grip.

"You fear nothing more than dreams!" Dels continued. "I wish nothing more to do with your madness!" Abruptly he turned and fled the room.

Rolind watched his brother leave. Then in the quiet of the early morn, as anger swelled within his mind, and while still tightly clenching all three pebbles in his hand, he peered down at the hopeless position of the ruby parrot by his foot and gave way to his deepest frustrations with a shout. Then with a powerful kick, he struck the wooden figures, sending them clanging across the marble floor, and while issuing a moanful groan, he too took to flight, leaving behind the overturned pieces and the disorder of a game in which he saw his life.

ii

THE CORRIDORS SEEMED ENDLESS; the galleried walls of prints and oils passed undefined behind a veil of tears as Rolind fled through his private chamber door. Hurriedly, the tortured youth traversed the room of shelves and books, mementos of distinguished guests which hung upon the walls: tapestries and flags, sabres, skins of furious beasts which roamed on distant shores, and images engraved on camphor wood, priceless scenes of glory. Even the golden harp, his one love beyond all, passed as though a blur within his mind. He found himself before the obiel and, pushing out the glass-paned frames, stood alone, enraged, demanding that the nightmare stop.

Moments passed and soon relieved of all those arguments of daggers, duels and death, Rolind stared across the light blue speckle-clouded sky until his senses returned, and he leaned against the rail, now conscious of the looping gulls flying white against the thousand feet of palisade before him, dropping down to cross the four-mile-wide hump-backed rift of land which rose into the pinnacle upon which the castle stood. Then freely flying high above the warm blue waters of a gentle sea which washed the beaches white, they floated out beyond a chain of tiny islands and finally disappeared from sight.

In a daze, Rolind crossed the room, and resting easily upon his bed, his chin against the harp's long gentle slope, he plucked upon the lowest tones a song of tears.

"YOU PLAY AS THOUGH the instrument is part of your being."

The words awoke the youth and he turned abruptly to cast away the voice. But as the deep gentle tones continued, the boy explored Tyre's flat wrinkled forehead and the strong angular features of his face.

"You play the harp as though you had been born with it, as though the student has long become master of the teacher. Perhaps there will come a day when you will realize that truth, and I shall be cast away."

Rolind searched the white-haired man's eyes and lips, seeing the gentle man who generated love. And dare he reveal that inner sorrow for all the world to see, Tyre would surely raise his long agile fingers and catch the tear.

"Nonsense, Tyre. You will always be dear to me. I shall never send you away."

"Then one day you shall be as old as I and we will laugh about your youth."

Rolind looked down at the old man's sandals, then quickly up.

"I fear now that my days are few."

"Why say you such a thing?"

"Could you not feel my sorrow in the music?" Rolind faced the sitting man. "I dreamed of death and spoke it with these strings."

"You cannot speak of things which are not real."

"But they will be, and too quickly, so I fear. And though you too pretend, I will not accept your comfort!"

"Perhaps then it is my age which makes me senile."

"How can you lie to me? Is such deception what you call . . ." Rolind hesitated at the echo of his brother's recent words. "When Dels accuses me of such an action I feel guilt. Are you so different as to be devoid of these feelings?"

Tyre remained still, staring into the boy's eyes.

"Even in this moment of silence I can read your thoughts, Tyre. There *is* murder in our future and it shall be *my* hand that lands the dagger."

"Does not your harp bring peace into the universe?"

"Oh, Tyre . . . it isn't fair to speak of other things. I need a way to abate my most dreaded inner thoughts, a plan to escape from the reality which certainly I face."

"A special music which comes from your harp . . ."

"Stop it! Stop it! You are torturing my mind!" cried Rolind, and he leapt off the bed to shout at his mentor.

"The only reality which you can know is that of the present," Tyre continued with a reassuring voice.

Rolind shook his head violently, waving frantic hands before the old man.

"What do you mean? You know as well as I, or any in this land, that my father condemns me pluck my brother's life! I cannot ignore that fate. In my eighth year dancers enacted our future to the universe and I heard five hundred voices bemoan the words which I have read and reread every night for seven years. How dare you deny this truth and speak so easily of other things? Oh, Tyre, this situation wears away my peace."

"Rolind . . ."

"No! You cannot deny it. I know. And you, Tyre, you are the only one to whom I can turn. Father always seems ready to cry, Dels fills me with such great apprehension that I cannot treat him well. And Mother, . . . Oh, Tyre, I miss her so. I miss her touch. I miss the games she would play upon my toes, her songs, her common sense. She has become so distant from me. No more does she kiss my forehead and tell me things for little boys; no more does she sing me songs. This most gentle woman spends her days locked away and, in her moments with us, avoids my eyes. And none can tell me that it is my sudden surge of puberty which has caused all this! She's much too strong for tears, but I feel them all suppressed. Tell me if you dare that these perceptions are wrong! Tell me if you dare that I can only know the present and that no future will exist!"

The ancient teacher answered in a quiet tone. "No good can come to speak of darkest things when beautiful objects still long their life."

"Do you deny my future?" Rolind turned away annoyed, facing the blank wall opposite the shelves, staring at the dark-stained table and the open book, wood- and leather-bound, pages of softest parchment. A wide orange candle resting in its cylindrical holder lit the words upon those sheets.

"Perhaps you wish to spare me from the pain." Rolind approached the book. "Or perhaps it is *your* way of denying what is obvious to all. But *I* cannot ignore that truth!"

"Rolind, please . . ."

"No! I shall read it to you, just as I once listened to those five hundred voices so many years ago."

"Rolind, don't."

The boy stood before the lighted candle and slowly read . . .

From much blood, from the deaths of Nju
and Klisd, there rose the family of which Byui was
head,
and with him stood his son, Kil:
and Byui was king of Meru til he died.

And Kil ascended to the throne
and there amidst great jubilation and feasting
the crown rested upon his head
and declared him rightful king o'er Meru . . .

And by his woman knew three sons
yet as though the rhythm flowed within his heart, Kil
spake:
"Only one true pollen shall produce the line to serve,
and Ghia, wife of Kil, will bear me sons no more."

"But what will happen to Awio and Trux, youngest
sons of thine,
conceived before the pledge?
for hold they not the yearnings of imperial right within
their *Li?*

would they not seize upon their nature and bring storms
of death and echoes of their father's proper place
within the universe,
and perhaps open infectious wounds upon the infant kingdom . . .

"They shall be kept in secret of their father's station
and be learned in the respect of Fre and all the princes
which descendeth from his seed."

And a moan stretched across the kingdom
from a father suffering from his greatest loss.

Awio and Trux were sent to Nmes and Iopes
to become men of learning
without their *own* knowledge
and to praise the ground of others entrusted with their care . . .

At Nmes and Iopes grew they stoutly into statesmen,
boasting clear voices and oration of the finest wisdom;
but in their hearts a silent yearning grew.

Great trouble brewed within their hearts
and Awio slew Trux . . .
and fled amongst the tribes to raise an army of ten thousand
to slay Fre, his brother, and claim the crown as justly his.

Fre with but a dagger in his hand,
and within the castle walls
met the rage of Awio covered with the blood of Trux.
"I have come for what is mine," Awio declared,
though ignorant of purpose with his blade,
and attacked the king with plan to see him dead.

But the tip did miss its mark
and the hands of Fre felt Awio's warm blood
and looked into his face to see great contentment
as death betolled his brother's life.

And thousands lay in graves,
But Fre did lay the seed to serve all Meru
and none had voice to raise.

"Rolind! Stop! It is only history you read."

"It is my future! Always has it been the custom for the king to sire only one son. Not since the days of Fre have two pretenders stood before the throne."

"Do you believe your father would sacrifice his sanity for history?"

"He would guard this kingdom with the very might with which he oversees it. If you were he, Tyre, who would you have chosen, Awio or Trux? Or would you have sacrificed one son and avoided destruction of what the king swears to perpetuate? Both Dels and I are equal before the throne and Father must make a choice."

"Rolind . . ."

"You hesitate to admit the problem and aim to appease me in the face of death!"

"Stop! You mustn't torment yourself in this manner."

"Why not? Could there be any peace in my life, knowing how fate defines my future? Perhaps I could hide it all away like Dels, but to what purpose is a quiet torment? My manner may be screams and protests, but perhaps it will eventually drown my thoughts. I cannot lock it up inside and deny the truth!"

"You so oftentimes repeat, *perhaps* . . ."

Tears flowed from Rolind's eyes. He drank them, powerless to restrain the frustration deep within.

"I become confused when the future appears so certain and none dare acknowledge it. I beg for aid, but receive nothing in return."

"But I can only offer you nothing. I have no answers for your fears."

Rolind stopped and stared, disbelieving the mentor's words. "Tyre, I can almost accept the emotions of those around me, but I will not tolerate lies and deceit!"

The white-haired teacher remained silent for a moment, as though in deepest thought for an answer to Rolind's words, then looking away into the bright sunlight beyond the obiel; he led the prince's eyes out beyond the room. Then he slowly rose and left.

Rolind looked out once again across the rippling waves. White pelicans dove into the green shoreline waters, then climbed high above the steep wall of rocks across the way. There Rolind's vision became transfixed upon the palisade edge, envisioning upon it the images of distant friends working in the fields of corn, their warm smiles beckoning him to declare within his inner mind, *"Escape from there and make the home of Citu your very own, and declare your field of corn your reign."*

And he turned and fled.

iv

ROLIND'S PATH along the castle corridors had been well worn by nine years of travel and the youth moved swiftly, ignoring the possibility of meeting guards or members of the royal family, descending into the lowermost level of the castle, where bare boulders of its ancient construction remained exposed. In the rough mortar he placed tender fingertips, and rotating a boulder around its hidden hinge, he exposed a dark hollow passageway down which he shimmied, finding little difficulty in sliding through. The boulder swung back, immersing the prince in darkness.

When first he had discovered the passageway, Rolind had imagined a hundred princes before him escaping from the castle to play games beyond its walls, yet oftentimes he wondered why his father remained ignorant of the path, never once hindering the boy's exploration of the maze.

Quickly he reached the flat surface below, shivering slightly, and though still in complete darkness, he ran at a rapid pace along straight corridors and around blind corners. One sharp edge brushed his palm and he winced in pain.

During the prince's eighth year he had discovered the strange black world below the castle. His moves, initially less quick and quite cautious, demanded laying yarn from his mother's knitting basket and adding to its length whenever he dared venture deeper below the surface of the mountain. And though he had searched with candles for some inscription or intelligent clue to aid in solving the mystery of the maze, the walls remained barren, save for their thick, undisturbed layers of dust.

The long corridor ahead of Rolind plunged sharply downhill and he ran even faster. Some turns took Rolind uphill, then spiraled him downward; some backtracked parallel to a previous direction, only to lead the boy in a totally unpredictable direction.

He had long since dispensed with the yarn, not because he feared detection of the game, but because it had ceased to serve in any way: the mere solution of the problem had become excitement enough for the royal child, and many times he would enter the dusty world of darkness just to test his memory.

But for the moment Rolind remained unconcerned with amusement, his eyes strained to see, his hands and fingers waved ahead, searching for tactile clues to reveal the next move. Soon, the boy-prince thrust out his palms and forcefully rammed against the wall before him, recoiling off the hard cold rock, dropping to his hands and knees and pushing against the lowest boulder. The stone rotated around a concealed hinge.

Sunlight pierced his eyes, and the youth shut his lids to accustom himself to the blinding sun. Then, he swiftly closed the passageway behind.

To reach the base of the steep pinnacle upon which the castle stood required running through the thick bushes of shrub oak and among tall Joshua trees. The salty brine from the vast blue sea tickled Rolind's nose and his rhythmic motion carried him by trees, around clusters of delicate purple flowers and over stumps and rocks. Soon the brittle trees led to patchy grass, then to coarse rocky sand to which the youth fled, becoming lost in the monotonous landscape surrounding his royal home. A bright sun had long arisen from its bed, and flooded the parched, bare land with a harsh white heat.

At the end of the hill, where the flat city began, Rolind stopped by a cluster of six tall Joshua trees. From one which had been hollowed out by death, the prince extracted a disguise: faded blue- and white-striped pants and a loose-fitting dirty white shirt. He quickly changed costume, even abandoning his soft, finely cut antelope sandals for the heavy striped leather ones common to youth in the kingdom of Meru. Draped in such a manner he was free to roam the streets and pass himself off as a merchant's son, or the lowest of lows—a street-sleeper who begged for alms.

The prince quickly entered the crowded streets of Meru, skipping along the twisting streets of single-story adobe walls, his manner carefree, only cautious of donkey-driven carts or other mundane dangers which might appear. He saw no images of the fearful dagger here and heard no haunting death-throes from his brother's throat. Carts laden with clanging pots and bouncing crates passed him by and the playful shouts of children further divorced Rolind from the castle's gloom. He ran among the shadows on the east side of the rough cobblestone street, his eyes careful not to peer into the open wooden doors and windows along the way, lest he be mistaken for a thief and sent before the King.

Soon the cobblestones led to a small open field, and a wooden fence separated the centrally located marketplace from the city streets; there he heard the feverish pounding of congas, sticks and wooden reeds, and saw tiny children bouncing like monkeys to the steady beat, and crippled beggars singing out for alms. A tiny boy danced hand-flips around the prince, and Rolind, feeling his newfound freedom, laughed, skipped around the field, and matched the urchin's tricks until he finally slipped and fell before the clapping crowd. His face grew red, the crowd cheered and Rolind smiled up at the child who bowed most gracefully before him, then bounced away, and was lost within the crush of onlookers.

Rolind rose and, smiling, entered the deep shade of colored tarps. Shouts of women selling wares and chattering amongst themselves filled his ears. Each sat upon a decorated rug displaying fruits, fish, cloth, dyes, sassel, clay and wooden wares. A thousand, so it seemed, brushed by the youth while the smell of spices and meats blended with the odor of human sweat and the chatter of individuals merged into a deafening drone.

A man rushed by the prince, yelling at some fleeing urchins whom he threatened with a stick. Rolind searched around for the merchant's empty stall and, rushing to it, grabbed a loaf of bread and two goose eggs, and abruptly disappeared into the crowd.

When he was safely on the other side of the market, he traded the raw eggs for some boiled veal, and while preparing to leave the old lady with his bargain, Rolind noticed the form of an old tobacco merchant, rocking in his wooden chair, puffing out thick white clouds of smoke and grinning at him from wide green eyes. Cautiously he approached this curious man who had carefully displayed his stock of broad brown tobacco leaves upon an ancient white rug. The wrinkled coffee-colored face seemed most entertained.

"What visions grow within your smoke, *cashi?*" Rolind said to the old man in a voice just loud enough to be heard above the crowd.

"A thief."

Rolind froze in his steps and stared into the man's powerful eyes.

"A young thief though; a most humble one."

"A-and where is he now?"

"In this pipe. I can see him now." He removed the stem from his mouth, blowing out a cloud of smoke. "Here, I offer you a look."

Rolind accepted the long curved stem, and placing the small carved bowl in one hand, he puffed three times and returned the pipe. A smile drew across his face as the tobacco played within his brain.

The old man said gently, "If a man offers one and you take three for greed, what pleasure exists in the offering?"

"But I pay you with my pleasure and thank you with this bread," Rolind said, splitting the loaf in half and tossing one piece toward the rocking man. "Now we are equal thieves, for you have stolen the perfection of my crime."

The old man laughed. "So it be, *lini.* Now run to the shade of a solitary tree and enjoy your prize. And hurry, or the lightness of this tobacco will fly away from you."

Rolind smiled gleefully and ran through the crowd, out of the market and over the round cobblestones, stopping beneath the shade of a tree which grew where no rocks lay and where none with words could disturb his dreams.

There the soft bark made a fine backrest and Rolind nibbled at the fresh crusty bread. Some small birds picked at the falling crumbs with long yellow beaks, hopping near the boy, searching feverishly for more. His mood remained dreamy, softly singing as two old men dressed in white cotton and carrying a mandolin and flute nodded at his smile as they passed. Rolind watched them stop before a wooden door, listened as they chortled a light folksong, then looked away as a moustachioed man surrounded by small urchins invited them to disappear within, gently closing the tall, brown door.

A rare breeze brushed Rolind's hair and he looked up suddenly to stare at the rectangular castle on the hill. Noon light reflected off its smooth adobe walls and the three levels of obiels pulsated, beckoning Rolind to explore the personalities deep inside.

Behind the left obiel sat his mother locked within the royal chamber, wailing with perpetual sorrow, her face buried behind rapidly aging fingers. And Dels appeared in the middle room, sitting quietly within his cloistered world of books, denying fate behind the fictional truth spun by other minds. And beyond the eastern windows flickered the perpetual candle revealing those words from the Book of Orange, vivid for a moment to this unhappy mind. Then he saw into the second level where his father sat in council, encircled by four men cloaked in flowing orange robes, mute yet stern, as though statues, unconcerned and blind.

Then the box-shaped hollowed-hall structure exploded with a roar; white boulders hurdled through the sky, racing towards the youth, then transformed into pieces of the game: the black panther clawing at his face, the ruby parrot cawking out with deathly gags, Dels' denials filling his ears, then a dagger red with blood drawing across his eyes . . .

Rolind rose and screamed at those images which raged within his mind and shouted to the air, "Of course it's true." He screamed, "It isn't fair to lie!"

The sun beat down and by its strength his madness grew. The cobblestones pressed against his sandaled soles, then tripped his feet, and threw the frenzied youth against a chalky wall.

Sweat beads formed—pulsations of his brain-blood pounding in his skull; a buried face to hide away the scene, a pause for tears quickly wiped away, then numbness and a stare. And there he lay, too weak to move, too afraid to dream.

V

Lying over the center of the land rib which divided the city of Meru into east and west, great fresh water springs and rivulets produced a rich, grassy grove, long preserved across the centuries as a sacred park called Gazebah. Here men studied the philosophy of *Li*, seeking peace from their most disturbing thoughts, reflecting on the purposes in life and seeking absolution for those who could not see.

Rolind eventually entered this realm of quiet, passing delicate flowers and tall wide trees, some of green foliage, others of dark red and violet leaves. Long black pod-shaped seeds loosely hanging from their dark black bark. The prince paused, feeling the heavy burden of his mind.

An old man adorned by a long flowing white robe halted the sorrow-filled boy and beckoned him to heed.

"Hurry not, *lini*. There grows peace around you. Come. Join us and let your sorrows fly."

Rolind stared into the plain golden locket hanging from the scholar's shoulders, then looked to where the wrinkled finger pointed.

"Thank you, *cashi*. It is hot and my thoughts are too heavy for me to bear."

The *Li Scholar* led Rolind to a circle of youths dancing between two red-leaf trees.

"If you play the lute, make us a song with ours. If not, then whistle a song declaring joy, and be welcomed in our dance."

Rolind hesitantly joined the circle but felt no less alone. Then, before any activity commenced, he joined the others in a singing lesson of the *Li*:

All bodies are one when
unified by touch.

All lives share one life when
each one shares his song.
From birth to death rejoice with
any other, for
There are no strangers in the
universe
But those who walk closed-eye
and closed-hand:
And there is no greater life than
one with all.

"Begin, *Kini,*" called out two smiling girls.

Rolind blushed, then looked around. A red bird with a black beak landed in the circle, then quickly flew away. The youth imitated the bird's high shrill. The others followed suit. A silence lasted and Rolind caught their curious eyes. He tried again but remained transfixed in the echo of the sound, feeling very much alone. A fleetng moment, and he looked up to the castle walls beyond.

"I am sorry," he apologized, breaking his grip from those who stood beside him. "But too much exists within my heart to celebrate with happy dance and song." And as he saw them still smiling, he ran to seek some other sanctuary.

Tears refused to flow and his rapid pace soon slowed to a shuffled walk. He focused upon the minute ripples of a treacherous sea, the leaves upon its waves like vessels under sail. The wind then carried up the shouts of men, a plea to have their wooden craft from the destructive storm. And he turned away with thoughts of running.

Before him stood a red umbrella tree, and within the subtle light of its wide shade sat a scholar who met his eye.

"Come and gently find your ease." The old man smiled and placed his book aside. "The grass is cool here and the wind blows softly."

Rolind thought to run, and though his feet began, his eyes inquired of the smile and he cautiously approached the gentle voice.

"Do deep thoughts swim within your mind?"

Roland surveyed the scholar's eyes and, finding peace, sat before the ancient form.

"How will I know if they interest you?" Rolind asked.

"Our words will flow as though only one voice speaks."

Rolind remained still, afraid to speak, and drawing his attention toward a dried red leaf, he raised it up and meticulously folded the slender form along its central vein.

"Tell me, *lini,* how do you envision life here in the days of Kil?"

The youth looked up, startled by the choice of words, but still suspecting this stranger's ignorance, he surveyed the pastoral meadow of trees and flowers.

"Perhaps it was as we find it in this Gazebah today. Although a new land then, with a breeze through every blade of grass and a bird on every branch." But as a vision of his father flashed before his eyes, he dropped the leaf and turned to face the ancient man.

"But then . . . such could never have been a real world, for it seems that all men are burdened with pain and sorrow. I question whether man has ever lived devoid of tears."

"Would those occupied with life bemoan their death?"

"But surely fathers have suffered, and surely so have their sons."

"And does a man who follows his *Li* suffer during life though he knows that death awaits him in the end?"

"The *Li?"* Rolind turned away, bitterly staring up at the castle behind him, then anxiously towards the palisades beyond his reach.

"What do you understand of the *Li, lini?"* The old man forced Rolind to return. "Do you know of its history and its purpose for each man?"

The young prince peered deeply into the ancient eyes, wishing to reveal what torment such knowledge had forever meant to him; but humbly he beckoned the scholar to speak, nodding a feigned innocence.

The *Li Scholar* touched his locket, then began.

"When Awio emerged from the vastness of the realm, discovering his true identity, and laid seige upon the castle of a brother he had never known, wise men contemplated his fate, concluding that some driving force had led Awio back to his natural domain. The ancient gods, Uno-pi and Lu-pi could not afford those scholars a resolution of the conflict raging within the man, for his actions had never been prophesied and did not fit within their ways as ruling gods. They surmised that Awio had been driven by a force deep within the very element of man, some inherent quality which would create the individual."

"But if the *Li* brings pain, does not a person know he follows the wrong path?"

"Of what subject do we speak, *lini?*"

"Of . . . of the princes, Rolind and Dels. Some say that one must die, while others disagree. I . . . I do not face murder," Rolind looked away, "but I love these two, such as speaks the lesson of the *Li*:

Make no tears of your own,
  but shed those made by other men;
For in their pain is the sorrow of the universe
  and in the cosmos are we one."

"And what knowledge have you concerning the royal lineage?"

Rolind plucked a blade of tall grass which grew around him, then looked up.

"Seven years ago dancers enacted the pain of our prince. Fate and five hundred voices moaned in assemblage those very words written in our sacred Book."

"Surely you were quite young, though most assuredly impressed by such a scene."

"But it was not that alone, for I stood in amazement, watching the Royal Horsemen break their play and drive these innocents from the Gazebah."

The *Li Scholar* smiled and nodded. "And do you therefore visualize the sorrow of the king?"

"But does the king suffer as do his sons, or does he merely act without concern for public politics?"

"And do his sons suspect this fate, and therefore suffer more?"

"If I were prince," Rolind avoided the old man's eyes, "surely I would suffer!"

"And would your father suffer should it be you who faced death?"

Rolind searched the palisade wall, forcing back the tears.

"Surely he would suffer most grievously . . . but he

would never permit it!" Rolind trembled as he confronted the moist, wide eyes before him, suddenly confused by the conclusions forming in his mind.

"Do you suggest, *cashi,*" he begged, "that the king is misguided, or have I been misled to such a conclusion? And if the king truly errs then no dual need exist. But who will save them? Or could it be that weakness overwhelms a teacher of the *Li,* and he, too, should lie?"

"And how do *you* resolve the conflict?" the scholar said, passing the problem back to Rolind.

"I take to flight!" he exploded, turning to face the north palisade, focusing his vision on the steep winding path which ascended the sheer wall. And he rose to speak while visions of the pending trek flowed before his eyes.

"I mean . . . I would probably flee away from here. Cautiously, yet steadily; to hide amongst friends and cast away my knowledge; to be resown where free from burden."

Then he faced the scholar, realizing that he had lost the feign with which he had begun. Surely there had been no restraint within his speech and Rolind now wished to quickly flee.

"It grows late, *cashi,*" he said. "And I have stayed too long, burdening you," he falsely smiled. "My words were nonsense and merely expressed for exercise."

"Even words spoken in jest will make one grow, *lini. Mali di.*"

"Mali di, cashi."

VI

ROLIND QUICKLY LEFT THE GAZEBAH, but the way seemed long and his aggravated fears diminished beneath a blazing sun as he sought diversions to pass the time. By the public fountains which lined the route, where fat women in colorful cottons gathered for water and gossip, Rolind drank deeply to refresh himself, listening amusedly to their birdlike chatter, and finally listening with a happy smile to secret woes and truths. Where the cobblestones rose high, he turned handstands and flipped around in an antic mood. A small scroungy pup followed for awhile, nipping at his toes. And when along the way a cart nearly ran him down, driving him against the chalky wall, the dog snuck between his legs, barking furiously at the inconsiderate lout. Yet further back beyond that spot, where no apparent danger lay, the dog suddenly fled, tail tucked between his legs, his ears pinned back. At first Rolind raced and shouted after the mutt, but the heat quickly exhausted him and he stopped. A noise suddenly startled the youth and he turned to discern the distant sound.

"Horses! Of course they are! The Royal Horsemen!" Who else could ride so swiftly and undauntedly disturb the afternoon stillness? The prince cautiously stepped back two paces, hoping to view the animals and know their purpose. But the road twisted too sharply and only the endless white adobe walls remained in view.

Father must have sent them. His mind raced with fear, turning away from the pounding steel hooves, searching for a place to hide. Then fleeing till he found a door, and amidst the deafening roar, he pounded fiercely against the hardwood barrier, rudely enough to disturb the deepest sleep and pain his slender hands.

"Let me in! Let me in! Let me in!"

Finally the door creaked open and Rolind leapt in, frantically squeezing his lean torso through the narrow slit, and with the same motion pressed back against the heavy timbers and slammed the great door shut.

There he stood, the echo of charging steeds deafening him with the clamor of steel and cobblestones. His eyes sealed shut with fear and his cheeks contorted in pain, waiting for those murderous creatures to drive their weight against his slender form and crush him lifeless against the door. And before him stood an image of his father, wide-eyed and angered, and the thunderous explosions of steel and rock beyond the timbers became the king's words to kill his son! Rolind shook his head, denying all which passed.

Finally the turmoil ceased and nothing but the steady beat of his heart echoed in his ears.

"Are you more at ease, *lini?*" A tender voice flowed in.

Rolind looked up to see his hostess: gentle, gleaming eyes and soft skin. She touched his hair. The boy bent over and clasped his knees, relieved from fear.

"Has the thunder left your ears and your eyes now free of demons?"

Her words startled him, but the youth looked up and feigned a smile: "It is just the heat, *nsamia.* It has rattled my mind and made me sensitive to common things."

"Such violence would tremble any man, and yet you be a youngster. Does not your mother worry when you walk the streets alone?"

Rolind avoided his tale of woe, and looked beyond his hostess' eyes to where three small children stood huddled together across the small open courtyard space, returning his curious stare. "She has as much concern for me as you have love for yours," Rolind said cautiously.

The woman raised her hand to lay flat the boy's long black flock of hair, then gently touched his nose, melting away his stoic stare.

"They are gone now, *lini.* Come in and refresh yourself, this heat is strong and our well is never dry."

Rolind followed his hostess across the courtyard, passing three short, stubby trees boasting coarse-skinned fruit and studied the rooms surrounding the open court. The corn room appeared half-filled and the four bedrooms revealed a family of ten. A cool breeze fluttered the leaves around them, refreshing the wary youth.

As they reached the stone well which stood opposite the entranceway, the children cautiously approached and small chickens crossed their path, pecking at the pebbled ground. Then a small, spotted dog charged after the red-frocked fowl and the children gave up their questioning stare to chase the mutt around. Rolind laughed. Then as one tyke tripped across his sandaled feet, he scooped the small boy up, and happily observed the woman smile.

"What is your *Li,* young man? You show such great gentleness for my child. Perhaps it be a teacher of the youth."

"I am a harps-player, *nsamia.*" He placed the tiny tot down and searched her face.

"A harps-player, so I swear!" he shouted out as though it were his sire who stood before him now. "I wouldn't lie to you!" He stepped back with every word. "I wouldn't lie, I swear!" he shouted, blind behind a veil of tears.

Suddenly her gentle touch lay upon his shoulder and though Rolind shook with fright, her manner touched his mind and the youth relaxed.

"Surely you do play the harp." She held his hands in hers. "Your sensitivity of mind is just as fragile as these fingers which must pluck the strings. And to dare the heat of noon must prove you the master of your art."

Rolind slowly relaxed, suddenly aware of his outburst, and stuttered out an apology.

"Can you predict the *Li* of your own children, *nsamia?*" he asked, fighting to suppress his tears.

The woman spoke in gentle tones. "My oldest five now express their *Li,* having found their way within the poems *Li Scholars* read. But these children," she pointed to the urchins by her feet, "are yet too young. But by his manner I know the *Li* for the one over there." She pointed to a small, thin child rolling a red ball to his sister.

"Which poem is it?" Rolind asked with great curiosity.

The woman smiled and spoke:

"Cast gold into the ground to be corn
and corn into the mouths of children

and children onto the land
to learn of life."

Rolind smiled at the thought, for it was to this *Li* which he walked.

"Surely does he love the world of soil and shall become a farmer as his uncle is. The other boy that you held shall become a merchant, so I believe, for he loves the motion of his arms and legs and forever searches into things. And the girl over there shall marry with an architect, for she is sensible and demands great beauty and rewards."

"It would be most amusing to know for certain their futures and compare them with your thoughts."

"But surely, *lini,* such knowledge must be kept a secret or these children would be without surprise in life and find no enjoyment in the poems recited by the scholars of the *Li.*"

Rolind smiled, and the gentle woman led him to the well where she withdrew the pail and offered him a drink. The youth drank deeply.

"You seem much more at ease, *lini.*"

"Yes, I am. This diversion has enchanced my joy and I may walk in peace. Besides, it grows late and I have far to go."

"Then take these bits of *guaya* from our tree for refreshment along the way." She plucked a tough-skinned fruit from a tree nearby, and on the table in the dining space next to the wall, sliced it small.

"There is only one fountain before the palisade and the sun will burn fiercely today," she said as she led him by the shoulder to the door.

"Mali dia, nsamia," Rolind spoke before he turned away.

"Mali di, lini."

VII

THE NORTH PALISADE ROAD scorched pale throughout the daylight hours, twisted flush against the shear wall of jagged rock fragments, and steadily rose a thousand feet. As Rolind began the trek, song was companion to the boy and he whistled freely, making the sharp turn along the way and counting the levels which he scaled. The city down below widened out—a mosiac of flat white rows and long grey shadows, delineated by twisting, snakelike streets, and here and there the blue-green shimmer of an emerald park. To the southeast Rolind could see the brown rectangular jetties built out from the beach and two ships rocking rhythmically just beyond the shoreline, obviously anchored in the bay, devoid of sails. A third ship glided effortlessly across the gentle waves to approach the port. Beyond the sea heavy clouds gathered in the west, but too far away to cool the sun. Vultures circled above the path, and as the heat quickly destroyed his ease, the joy of climbing became a burdensome task.

Even the road seemed to turn against him. Hot sands sifted between the flexible straps of his sandals, chafing the tender skin, making Rolind wince with pain and curse the deafening solitude. Jagged pebbles stubbed his toes and his cotton shirt swelled heavy with sweat, chafing and burning the reddened skin along his neck. Rolind feverishly sucked the pieces of *guaya,* extracting from the yellow fruit its thick sweet pulp; but soon all was gone. He cursed with scowling lips the revolving shadows of vultures overhead, shouting out defiance at their death-wish dance, then rubbed a hand across his forehead to draw the slippery blanket of sweat down to his lips and taste its warm, salty liquid, sneering at the menace of death.

In his torment vision grew. First came undefined shadows of his greatest fears, then gaping jaws to fill his brain with screams in coarse jabbering static. Watered eyes swelled with anger, and suddenly came the noise of a rhythmic beating. Horses!

Rolind turned abruptly.

"Horses! The horses return!"

Armored steeds came billowing huge clouds of dust behind them, choking the boy with hot, heavy breaths, driving him back up the path; the echoing laughter of mounted riders pierced his brain, making him fold his frail arms across his black eyes to block out their sight. Then he screamed out violently, shaking his head in utter disbelief. And finally he fell before it all, his mind a wide chasm, hollowed out with fear, a hysterical mass of protoplasmic rock buttressed as though incapable of human pain.

But nothing touched his being save the deepest silence of his mind. Swaying helplessly from side to side, he capitulated to the fluid sway of limp arms and weakened thighs, dropping on his back, suddenly aware again.

And soon again he climbed, whistling and gay, free from madness, so it seemed, stepping with a skip.

But then he was once more a figure frantically kicking loose soil and shouting in his mind.

"No, Father! Don't you understand my fears . . . don't you see any other purpose for my life than death? . . . I can almost laugh . . . I beg you, declare this madness, folly, and say it done. . ." he begged, swinging sightless eyes along the ground. "Can't you see us as your sons, to love, not to murder? Must you give us weapons made for death? Is that our sole *Li* in life, to kill ourselves. Please," he begged, "let our nature make one king." Then his steps played out the rhythm of his hate. "Do you admit no love in your heart!" he shouted at the imaginary man. "Have you only honor and sentiment to some mystical past!" His cheeks swelled painfully, his hands waved frantic pleas: a silhouette of madness. Then a dagger thrust into his brother's chest: Dels shrieked in pain and Rolind screamed.

Raising up a jagged rock, he crashed it to the ground. A gray-brown storm flew up, driving off a peaceful bird along the precipice. Rolind watched it fly until the orange wings passed the royal castle and there his stern gaze was fixed. Tears flowed on, sounds of muffled frenzy filled his ears and Rolind stood, maddened on the edge. No longer could he speak nor scream nor see beyond his tears, and his rage became a single beat.

Soon the sun cast the tears into a salty skeleton, which needle-pierced the skin below his eyes. Rolind looked away. Then he stepped beneath the shadow of an overhanging ledge, relishing its shade and relaxing in the darkened coolness of the road.

There in the wedge before him, where the light-hued sky fused into the motionless sea, images formed of freshly turned furrows, moist and fertile fields, tall waving stalks transformed into a golden rug of corn, waving like the strings upon his harp, casting him into a wondrous dream, at peace within his home and amongst dear friends. Relaxed against the smooth rock along his back, his head nodding gently with the breeze, Rolind watched the subtle colors change before his eyes, then closed both heavy lids and in this ease fell fast asleep.

The sun continued traveling further west. The shadow under which he lay crept eastwardly, exposing the youth to the sun and destroying that tranquility of sleep. His yawn was quick and as he rose realized what distance lay ahead and he looked back, hoping that a cart might come and take him to the top.

His climb now steady, Rolind continuously peered below. Meru seemed a uniform mass broken only by the speckled green of parks and the plushest Gazebah. Even those small islands lying to the north appeared as flattened discs against the sea, a ship upon the waves appeared an illusionary thing, and the sun, it seemed, flew quickly by.

A whistle of air broke the silence and Rolind noticed a boulder split wide along its bulk. Then spotting a familiar, brittle, leafless tree growing out beyond the base of another stone, he hurried along. Suddenly he stood afront a wide semicircular gorge clean-fallen from the rocky edge, and there he knew that road's end was near. Though his thighs were knotted and tired, Rolind continued to ascend, and before he could find expression for his joy, he turned abruptly with the road, headed south and passed through a narrow corridor lined by steep gray boulders. The sea and the castle lay behind him.

Here the path rose even more steeply than before, but the moist refreshing breeze cooled his forehead. Solid rock slabs became soft brown soil and he whisked past overhanging branches and soft grass. Rolind skipped and smiled and slapped the muddy wall, then emerged into the subtle shadow of an ebbing sun. The coarse, rocky road softened beneath his sandaled feet and the land around appeared flat and green with corn. A gentle breeze carried the odor of lush wet soil into the air and he skipped, enshadowed by tall, green trees along the road, careful not to step upon the small white sunspots cast sparsley through the dense dark leaves.

viii

THE ROAD RAN STRAIGHT, and deep shadows stretched across the fields and the high-flying vultures had disappeared. Here his pace accelerated, for he hurried to the home of Citu. The breeze blew briskly for awhile, refreshing Rolind from his arduous climb, and he stared across the fields, watching men and animals prepare to leave their work. Citu's fields lay on the southeast side of the road beyond a house which Rolind could not yet see. Only half an hour remained before the heavy shadows came. The sky would still remain a pastel hue until the sun could complete its full arc across the city far down below.

He reached a tree, bleached white with death, its bare and outstretched arms a ghostly frame in the twilight, and he smiled at the familiar sight. But before he could complete the last few hundred feet to Citu's house, a grey donkey blocked the way, a young boy beaming down from atop the wooden seat. The prince pulled the donkey toward him by its sassal reins and slapped the gentle creature beneath its neck.

"How are you, Njii?" he greeted the boy, forcing a smile.

"Ah . . . Evan." The youngster addressed the prince by his alias. "You return as usual. Have you come for good, or shall we have to meet you here again?" Reaching down, he gently tugged at Rolind's long black hair. "Ah, Evan," continued the young philosopher, "you are truly a strange one. Content one moment in Citu's fields, then just as quickly gone. Will you ever be at peace, my friend?"

The prince looked curiously at the boy, for he had thought none could see his deepest fears. "It seems, Njii, that you have worked in the fields today," he said, touching the boy's mud-caked white cotton clothes and bare dark toes. Fresh, thick mud still hung from Njii's leather soles.

The boy quickly dismounted and offered Evan his seat. "And I am sure that you have walked far, Evan. Here."

Rolind gladly accepted the mount and smiled as Njii tugged the sassal rope drawing the creature along, the wooden slabs of the saddle clammering in the sway as Rolind's legs limply rocked below.

"When you have come to stay, Evan, this animal will be yours."

"And then, how will you get around, Njii?"

"I shall walk as you do now, to discover the land of which you speak, where giant men are parrots and love to eat snakes. Then perhaps I will board a sailing ship and discover a thousand other marvelled things."

Then Njii guided the beast onto a side path from which Rolind could finally catch sight of Citu's thatch-roofed home.

"You have grand plans for one so small, Njii," Rolind answered the dark-tanned youth. "Would your mother not worry were you to go so far?"

The youngster looked up with a grin. "No more than yours." He answered as the beast stopped a few paces before Citu's door. "Here we are. Now I must hurry off home."

Rolind dismounted, and as Njii sat upon the saddle, he looked down and spoke. "I know you leave tomorrow, for you are always saying 'goodbye.' But have no fear: upon your return I shall be on the road to greet you. *Mali di,* Evan."

"Mali di, lini."

ix

"EVAN HAS COME! Evan has come!" a small girl shouted from the courtyard. Four children quickly ceased their game of catch, and as they greeted him the chickens filled the center square.

"Come join us in our game," called a boy about eight years old, throwing the visitor a large knotted rag.

"Yesterday in school a boy named Sidi captured an *anesu* winding on its belly through the room," Anil continued as though the newly arrived guest had never been away. "Then we milked his venom and played with him."

"Were you not frightened, Anil?" Rolind asked, as they crossed the hard-caked yard.

"No, for we stuck soft gum into his mouth. His fangs were useless, then."

"And what did you do with such a dangerous catch?" he inquired of the child.

"The teacher had us kill the viper, for his poison would surely return and make the serpent a menace to our elders in the field. Have you come to help Citu with his corn?"

"I cannot say just yet. Does he still drive his plow? The sun is almost down."

The odor of stewing tomatoes enticed the youth's senses, and with the group of urchins still tugging at him, Rolind approached the cooking room opposite the door, passing by the small disordered sleeping rooms to his left. A large, soft woman looked up to shine her flush red cheeks at him, and though she smiled, she continued with her work. Rolind watched her stir a thick red sauce and add to it diced yellow, green and purple spice. A girl of thirteen sat beside the busy woman kneading yellow corn dough between her palms; then she dropped the thick, wet batter upon a hot, flatrock slab. The meal hissed a moment, then quickly rose into a light, round bread. As the girl removed the crusty loaf and placed it beneath a towel to her left, she smiled up at Rolind and then ran swiftly past his embarrassed grin.

A small boy about four years old approached his chatting siblings, and after tugging strongly at Rolind's pants, he began to play a hand-carved recorder. All voices ceased, the children listening with glee. The tones came high-shrilled, but tender with visions of soaring doves and gliding clouds. When the child ended his melody, Anil broke in with words.

"We call *lini, cashi lipo,* master of the wind. "He has learned a great deal since you last visited us two months ago."

Then the pretty girl re-emerged from a distant room and approached the group, spreading out a white dress adorned with colorful flowers.

"And we now call Sasha, *cashia casuna,* mistress of nonsense."

The pretty dark-haired girl ignored the giggling children and smiled brightly into Rolind's eyes. The youth looked away.

"Evan," she cooed, "how do you like my new dress? Is it not a pretty one?"

Rolind nodded, red-cheeked.

"Mother and I made it, and I shall wear it on my wedding day." She stepped back blushing. "Will you be there?"

The jolly woman looked up quickly with a laugh. "Now, Sasha, come away. You speak nonsense. Evan has come to visit with Citu, not with you."

Sasha quickly folded up the dress and after returning it to her room, once again sat by her mother's side to knead the bread. With each slap she smiled at the nervous youth.

Then a call disturbed the scene.

"Evan, Evan! How good it is of you to come."

A youth of fifteen stood at the entrance to the yard, his white cotton clothes caked with mud and a broad smile gleamed beneath his wire-brimmed hat.

The urchins ran off to greet their brother and Rolind smiled back at his approaching friend. The two met in the center of the yard and stood in a welcome salute.

"Shall we retreat to my room and leave the women to their work and the children to their games," coaxed his friend across the yard, walking with him arm-over-shoulder. Quickly they disappeared into a chalk-white room.

Rolind felt at ease in that familiar space, quickly surveying the double-tiered bed which served Anil and his flute-playing brother above and Citu in the bunk below. Rolind ran his hand across the rope-strung pad. And to his right stood a small box beside the entranceway in which the brothers stored their clothes and toys. He sat by the table opposite the door, finding just enough room to stretch his legs.

"It has been a long time, Evan, much more than a month. How do you fare?"

Rolind forced a smile, though still feeling uncomfortable behind his lie. "It is fine in the city below, but extremely difficult climbing up the palisade."

"I am sure you suffer from exhaustion, for the heat is much too great for joy. We have had so little rain this month, barely enough to make our crops grow."

"I noticed how green the fields are, certainly a good sight."

"Evan, I must show you this." Citu hurried out the words and, kneeling on the floor, pulled a common cloth sack from beneath his bed and extracted an orange box from within the purse. His eyes gleamed as he revealed the box.

"It is beautiful, Evan, don't you think?" he said, handing the colorful object to his friend. The box fit easily within both hands and as Rolind surveyed the jewels and pictures in relief an excitement overwhelmed his mind.

"It is ancient, I believe," Citu continued. "And once part of a glorious hoard. This cover must be ivory." He pointed along the main relief. "And these, along its border, precious stones."

Rolind stared at the insignia upon the top—a black panther encircled by white rosettes—the ancient crest of Byui, reminiscent of the days when Awio slew Trux.

"And this frame is most surely cast of silver."

"And inside! Inside, Citu! What did you find?"

Citu looked up surprised at Rolind's sudden speech, but quickly placed mud-crusted fingers across the lid and exposed a ruby-lined interior and a small book, bound in black lanugo which he held easily in one hand.

"Look at it yourself, Evan. Its symbols are foreign and make no sense to me. I opened it once, but could not decipher it. Here . . ."

The prince caressed the plain black pelt, then carefully, anxious of the words he might find inside, opened the book. Then without awareness of his good friend's presence or of his departure, he read without a pause:

Today has been most sad. As I walked along the outskirts of the village, I found much destruction, and amongst the ruins, a hut within which a young girl lay. I had never seen her before. Her age I guessed no more than seven years. Blood flowed slowly from her chest and she seemed in so much pain that I did nothing more than hold her in my arms and watch the child die. As I lifted up her head, tearful eyes beckoned me to tell what great wrong had made her deserve such pain. I stroked her brow and told her, none. Perhaps she might have died more pleasantly, but it seemed a great battle raged within her heart, as though perhaps she had indeed lost something greater than her blood. I knew not what to do, yet could not leave the child alone. Then, as though a great wind had brought me the only beauty which I find within these violent days, Nja came upon me and the dying form, and with the strength which she has been to me and those with whom she meets, took charge. And though the child seemed closer to her death, Nja sang to her a gentle song. The girl looked softly into Nja's eyes and felt peace within her heart, rested back her head and died. We laid the child nearby a solitary tree within the burning field, and though I could not bear to speak, Nja took my hand and held it tight and told me peace would one day come.

The battles seem to rage without an end. Nja met me by the brook today. And though we tried to find some answer along its bank, too much blood flows within its bed. We came upon an older woman, much possessed. Yet when we spoke to give her comfort, she turned upon us and shouted us away. Behind her in a shawl I espied an urchin, and the woman threatened to end its life. I flew upon her, and holding her away, Nja snatched the child and brought it to her breast.

"Why have you set upon to do great harm to this child, old woman," I asked.

"Better that she die here beneath her mother's hand than suffer endlessly by men."

And then I knew she was not possessed, but fearful of the war, for she fell upon her knees and cried, and Nja told her, rejoice, for she would protect the child and take her to a safer place. Then peace seemed to descend upon the woman and, though confused, she implored we hide the child away and feed it on the sunlight every day. We took the child and straightaway made it ours.

Perhaps the time grows near. It is said that Fre has come to lead the army by himself. A great leader would he make. Hope grows throughout the land. Nja spends a great deal of her time at home. It is strange for me to see, for all this time it has been she who has given peace to those she meets. But this child has given her a greater ease and gentleness unbeknownst to me. Truly do I love her.

Today, although the news of Fre is good, I came upon two urchins both bleeding from the face. Their pain seemed great, but mostly fear caused their tears. Never have I seen such fear in all my life, but it seems to strike me most when I search their eyes. I could not leave them there to die, and carried them away. I do not know from where all these strange children come in recent days; perhaps I grow aware in sensing all their pain. Nja seems so happy with them and gives them all affection. The crying surely stops.

I brought home more children today. There was a little girl covered with mud and blood and she walked along as though blind. The boy named Ghiu speaks to her and they stand alone hand in hand. I am glad he brings her laughter in the day, but wish the others would begin to smile. Now there are seven of us, and great commotion fills the time. The children wear clean clothes, and although I see them stare into the void each night, fewer tears are shed.

The battle looks worse than ever, and the feeling throughout the village is that Fre might lose. It is such a pitying sight to see hollow men throughout the streets believing that the end is near and offering themselves nothing for purpose in this life.

It is as though life is over for me, for such sorrow swells as I never thought a man could feel. Never could I have known the suffering, what those children felt alone in every sleepless night. Here are words which are hard to speak. Nja is dead.

I set aside this day for gathering apples, for hunger daily grows. No great storerooms remain, most of our food having been destroyed and the rest given out to those who come begging at our door. But when I returned, gray smoke filled our fields and I hurried up to see, holding dear the precious fruit until my weakened grip relaxed and I let them fall upon the parched soil. On the path before the house Ghiu lay, and he was burnt, in greatest pain. I did nothing more than listen to his cries till I could no longer bear them, and though we had beeseched the older woman for nearly bringing death upon the child, I held the boy against my chest and brought him quickly out of pain. It felt so hard to sense him die within my grip and quickly did I run from him. Death does not appall me any more. Passing through the threshold of the house brought that sickness which I might have suffered from Ghiu's death, for upon the floor lay children dying in most horrible contortions. And I fearest most the scene which was assuredly within the smaller room. Though my stomach was sick and my mind weighted down with tears, I entered. And there she lay, Nja on the floor, the young child whom she had saved from the old lady clinging tightly to her breast. I could not stay within there long, and though my face felt ready to burst with tears, I did not cry, but rather led myself out beneath the sky, and shouted out for everything to hear.

I feel more at ease since Nja's death, though I doubt my love for life shall ever be reborn. I decided to leave our village and head for Decor and the River Corodo, but the trek was long and my mind could find no peace. The orchards are all charred and the stench of corpses reeks throughout. The war seems impossible for me to comprehend. Even those who pass speak of depressing things, and once again I can feel the hollow sense of absurdity about it all.

On the road an old man lay dying. I tried to aid and bring him comfort in his final hour. As I waited for the sage to die, Ghiu's image haunted me with screams of pain and I hid the sounds by questioning this man. Did he fear his death? He told me, yes. The sage soon died and I laid him to rest beside the road.

It is a pity to be a small man while others run your life. The road to Decor seemed long yesterday, but impossible today. There is nothing beautiful to see, the battles rage ahead. Along the way I heard a moan and turned to see a man lying in the marsh. I have grown hard these days and could feel no pity for this soldier. Yet as I approached he appeared no ordinary man. Beside him grazed a golden steed armored in the finest bronze, and he himself was dressed most nobly for a warrior. I fetched him water from the river and he did not mind its color, for he rested in a pool of thickest blood. I begged him tell me of the war and of its sense, and I might have killed this stranger when he laughed. But as he coughed I saw a great realization of his own impending death flash across his face. And still his tale filled me with so much anger that if he did not lie there doomed to die, I have might surely run him through.

He spoke of Awio and said that he was not *the son of Kil, being long ago killed in youth by Sepro, a second cousin of Klisd whom Byui had slaughtered for the throne. Then Sepro raised his own son, Casi, to call himself Awio, for he appeared similiar to Kil and sent him off to gain the throne and power for the family of Klisd. For the death of Fre, Casi would be king, and his father, master of the wealth. This soldier who lay before me had long been an aide of Sepro and helped him in his murderous deed. But Casi did not trust his laughter and his quiet way, and in the morning battle ran a lance into his lung.*

Oh, how mad it is, that Trux lay dead and Fre should duel a stranger who only shares his fate, and all around me lies such senseless, needless death.

From this soldier's hoard I took this jeweled box which Nja might have loved and set me off to cry.

Rolind closed the diary, his head tilted back, the story which he had just read spinning in his mind.

So, Awio was not driven by his Li, *but by a mere mortal's will . . .* realizing that the *Li* concept had been based upon false doctrine and that no predestined truth need make him fight his twin. His anxiety increased and he arose, ready to reveal it all to his father. But as he rushed for the door Citu blocked the way.

"Where did you find this, Citu?" Rolind demanded of his friend.

"With our corn full rooted and the furrows cut for rain, Jipolen and I drove our carts far south below the mountain's range to gather kindling wood. Amongst the oak groves at wood's edge this mound appeared where a fly amanita grew, and beneath it lay this box. I carried the treasure home to store common things which seem to me of great value. What does it say, dear friend?" he asked and sat upon the bed facing Rolind's distant stare.

Rolind looked away as though speaking to the wind. "It is written in the ancient tongue of Yiou taught to me in Gazebah one year ago. The pen speaks of deception in the realm of Fre when Awio and Trux defied the ancient pledge. But it was not a blood-line conflict as spoken in the Book of Orange, but conceived by strangers for wealth and greed." Roland turned to face his friend as his father's image flashed before his mind.

"Citu, may I carry this book with me to show my *Li Scholar*? He lies close to death. It would delight him to read these ancient words of history. I shall return it to you."

"Of course, Evan, this fine box is all I wish."

Rolind glided the book carefully into his pocket, smiling as he conjured up visions of great happiness about his throne.

"But tell me, Evan," Citu begged, "why did you come today? Before this moment I saw grief beneath your smile."

Rolind looked up, surprised by Citu's revelation. But a gentle rap on the door turned their heads. Sasha entered carrying a tray of steaming coffee and flat bread.

"You are hungry, Evan, and I carry you this before our meal," she said, placing it upon the table. Rolind smiled, nervously nodding approval of her presence there. The aroma of strong coffee enticed him to nibble at a pastry bit.

"Your chore is finished, Sasha," Citu reminded his sister. "Girls have no place beyond their duty."

"But it is my *pleasure,* not my duty, to serve Evan." She gazed toward the boy-prince. Amidst the giggles of children outside, she invited the guest to dine.

"It is not for you to invite Evan!" Citu snapped. "He has come to visit me. Now go away and bring his dinner! You act too foolish and make me ashamed of you." He closed the door behind his sister. Then Citu turned around. "Sisters! They are all alike. She is kind, of course, but too much underfoot. Now, here . . ." he said, and poured two cups of coffee.

Rolind sat back, his thoughts returning to those words he had found in the ancient diary, wishing to reopen the book again and reread those words within.

"And tomorrow, Evan, after you leave, shall we ever see your smile again?"

Rolind looked up, his thoughts invaded by his friend's voice.

"I must confess, Citu, I had come to you for aid, but now I'm not so sure. I sought a place to stay. Perhaps I could help you with the crop."

Citu smiled excitedly. "Of course! See this bed? it is half yours for sleep, and this thatched roof will shelter you as it protects Ciop, Anil and myself. And our food shall be shared with you, as shall our smiles and joy."

"I am most grateful, but I don't know if, or when . . ."

"There is no problem! It is already settled, and father shall sew you a pair of sandals for laboring in our mud." He rushed out, before Rolind could speak again.

Alone he sat, so alone, peering through the rooms' wide-open door, watching fluffy clouds pass on high. The evening silence carried aloud the companion song of donkey bray. Suddenly Sasha filled the space before his eyes, her deep smile of richest black relaxing him. And with gentle ease, she set the steaming food beside his arm.

"Here," she said, "to warm you deep," then she turned and fled.

II

i

THAT NIGHT Rolind slept fitfully: the story of Awio's deceit recurred within his dreams, and his imagination painted scenes of celebration throughout the land. And when he embraced his father, the man held high the ancient diary for all to see, proclaiming holidays for all to share his joy. When sleep finally overcame the youth, it ended soon and Rolind rose before the sun, careful not to awaken the sleeping Citu by his side, and quickly dressed. Assured of his possession of the book, he fled across the eastern palisade. Great excitement overwhelmed all sense and his feet made haste to leave. Some dogs rudely wakened by his noise quickly settled back to sleep. The brisk wind rustled through the row of trees along the road, and Rolind's skin was cooled by the moisture in the air. The beauty of young corn plants filled his eye and gray gliding clouds permitted only momentary glimpses of a phantom moon.

As the solitary chirp of a starling broke the lifeless night and announced the approaching sunrise, Rolind quickened his pace. Finally he reached the rocky apron of the palisade's edge and at a few hundred feet to his left came upon a high flat stone. Its center, worn by a hundred centuries of wind and rain, offered all those who stopped a most comforting repose—a common throne from which any man could watch the awe of nature's grace.

The day began.

A cap of light, a bright orange disc, arose from the deep blackness set beyond, coloring the sky along the sea, making it suddenly bright with blue. Small white-sailed fishing vessels bobbed upon the high sea waves, crossing afront the bright glowing sphere.

Rolind leaned back, content. A few raindrops struck a melody against the rock, then water doused his skin. The sky above appeared a quilt of gray and black and he quickly rose to rush along the steep cliff's edge and back to the road which would lead him down the steep palisade.

Against the darkened background an ass-drawn cart approached and Rolind waited on the road, recognizing it as belonging to Polin, a deaf-mute who drove the wagon painted bright with rows of multi-colored squares. Concentric colors circled the brass hex-nut of the solid wooden wheels. The driver slapped the solitary beast with reins of wide green suede, twisted and joined by large brass rings. The ass itself was donned with colored strips of finest leather. Bells clanged gently on its path.

Rolind greeted the driver with a waving hand and a joyful smile. As he slapped the donkey's buttocks and wiped away the mud, Polin laughed, saluting him with a red felt hat and revealing, with a sweep of his hand, an unoccupied portion of the water-soaked bench. Rolind returned the smile, then gladly climbed aboard. An old black long-haired dog nudged his way between the two and laid his soaking snout across the prince's lap. Rolind laid an arm across the mongrel's neck, rolling slippery fingers through its coarse wet fur. While the boy-prince settled comfortably across the wooden seat, Polin was reaching out, catching raindrops in his hand and offering Rolind a cool, refreshing drink. The two swallowed the delightful liquid. Then with a click from Polin's tongue, the cart lurched forward and Roland fell sharpy back.

They passed between a corridor of boulders, and turning north followed a path similar to the one which Rolind had ascended the day before. And because the rain stopped further down the trail, the warming sun had a chance to dry the tiny caravan. Rolind looked out towards the castle, anxious to reveal the treasure bulging in his pocket, spending each anxious moment in reconstructing scenes of celebrations which must surely come.

FOUR MILES FROM THE PALISADE and three from the castle the smell of brine and rotting fish filled the air. Seagulls cawked, swooping down and catching up unwary fish. Along the harbor boardwalk merchants exposed boxes of slippery silverfish, some still flopping under the intense morning sun. Polin's cart rocked up and over cobblestones, then smoothly upon the wooden docks. There he stopped the cart and Rolind jumped out, watching his friend click his tongue and move the cart away, down to an unseen jetty. The boy-prince peered back up at the east palisade, a smile drawing across his face, happy with his find. Then he walked among the chattering crowd, hurrying past a peglegged man, carefully avoiding the crippled smile and hard, coarse laugh. Fishmongers, their handcarts laden with fresh morning hauls, shouted for the boy to stand aside and let them pass.

Soon he reached the water's edge and there, upon a piling stump, sat to watch the rushing waves and feel their power sway the wooden dock. A gentle breeze blew by as Rolind took the diary out: its passages brought renewed relief and once again he conjured up the joy which his father would surely feel. Then hunger swelled his gut and Rolind rose to face a salty tavern across the wooden walk.

Effortlessly he swung the hinged doors, and was halted by the odor of beer, smoke and urine. And sliding his feet across the sawdust floor, he cowered beneath the hulks of boisterous men whose massive frames made the youth feel weak and small. Never had he dared to enter such a place before. Once had he heard that boys could earn enough coin to feed themselves, so Rolind traversed the hall trying unsuccessfully to avoid physical contact with the unruly crowd. When he reached the bar he looked up and peered into a gaping mouth of missing teeth.

"S-sir, I beg you let me carry beer to these men. I so badly need the coin and hunger makes my belly ache."

"You appear well fed and healthy to me," the gruff voice returned. "But any boy who dares enter this hole can try his hand. But I warn you," his eyes opening with great fury, swallowing Rolind's last bit of confidence, "no begging amongst these men or I'll split your jaw! Here! Take this tray of steins to them, over there, and be sure to collect the tab. Then go and let your worth be known!"

Rolind backed away, slowly at first, then hurried off to complete the chore. He tried to ignore the clamor all around him, but caught bits of conversation as he slid carefully through the crowd, collecting tips and carrying steins and rolls.

". . . Ay, she is a gilded dove whose thighs are so firm as to make any man's innocence glad to be away." The speaker suddenly grabbed Rolind's arm and spun the boy to face him. Rolind stared into a coarse stubbled beard and a row of broken teeth.

"Yeh, muffet, you too would find no greater pleasure in the universe then this whore's firm flesh," he croaked, and released the boy, his bellowing laughter echoed by his friends.

Rolind slunk away, trying to find a quieter place.

"Six ales. Here, boy!"

". . . and this king of ours . . ."

Rolind turned to face the muffled voice and set to wiping nearby tables.

". . . there are great numbers of men with weapons who feel deeply of this affair. Janil has six hundred men and Alwip three hundred. They sharpen swords and shoe their steeds. No king shall live to see his prince's death . . ."

Calls for drinks flew across the room, but Rolind stared fearfully at the man. This was a Kinu tribesman from the distant south, his long red hair knotted behind a huge round skull, bigger than most men's, resting on a powerful neck. Beneath the silk shirt Rolind could see a muscular physique which few would dare to challenge. As the Kinu raised up his stein to drink, Rolind spotted a black archer's gloves with the crest of Byui—a hired soldier, loyal above all else to the Crown.

". . . and you, Tasau, will you join us?" The man's voice rose as he lifted his ale.

"Hush, man!" came a subdued plea. "There are too many ears here. Already the Royal Horsemen and imperial spies have infiltrated the city."

"I don't care! These are words I speak without restraint!"

Others turned to face the Kinu. Rolind remained deaf to those who called for drinks.

"No so loud." His friend cast an eye upon the suspicious crowd. "Your death in a petty feud with ignorant men would be too great a loss."

"I fear no man!" came his powerful barked reply, as he pounded out defiance upon the solid oak.

Tasau clasped the Kinu's wrist, trying to hold it down.

"Hold me not, man!" He broke the grip with incredible ease, rising up before the onlooking crowd, and withdrawing his sword from its sheath. "Let *no* man here ignore the injustice within our realm."

"You are drunk," pleaded his comrade above the sudden silence, then turned to the others, smiling. "He is drunk, nothing more." But when none accepted the hint, anger swelled beneath his cheeks and with gritted teeth he sharply snapped at them. "He is drunk! Now look away!" as most yielded to his shout.

"I *am* drunk!" the Kinu shouted, "but not drunk enough to forget that our king does err should his thoughts stink with murder! This shield," he said, displaying the crested glove for all to see, "does protect not only the king, but *all* heirs to the throne! Can any man in Meru accept the death of any prince without emotion?"

"Stop it, Kinu . . ."

"Callio is the name, my friend. There is more hurt in my heart than the covering of my name could hide."

Rolind's stare caught Callio's eye, and standing in awe he watched the Kinu tribesman approach.

"What is my plea?" the soldier continued. "Could any of us sleep one night if this lad before us were our prince?" He paced the sword tip against Rolind's chest.

"And it was *his* blood which flowed within the imperial home?"

Rolind stared, terrified at the sword's edge, remembering the nightmares which had haunted him throughout the years. Then looking up into Callio's eye, he wished to reveal the true story of Awio and set this man's mind at ease. *But there is no bother now,* he thought. *I carry the diary and all this shall be done away with soon.* And when Callio withdrew his weapon and bowed his head in realization of the enacted deed, Rolind backed away, and quickly fled the scene.

HE RAN ALONG THE CROWDED DECK, recalling Callio's fear with every step, glad that he possessed the ancient book. With the few coins he had gathered in the bar and the lucky find of a silver one, Rolind bought some bread and wine and entered the park called Prebih. There he followed gusts of wind flowing within the maze of trees. The sound of jeering calls—children heckling something in their realm—made Rolind advance cautiously until he reached a small cluster of purple trees. And there he came upon a group of urchins dancing in a mocking way, tossing twigs and clumps of grass upon a screeching man. As the fifteen-year-old approached, the younger children fled.

There beside a tree Rolind found a crippled man, who walked upon his palms for he had no feet to wear away the sod. He wore on his head a black and yellow turban which boasted a stone of sylvanite for all the world to read. And he stared through spheres which had never known the shapes or colors of the universe. Yet with all these deformities, his mouth bore an enormous smile and his cheeks glowed with innermost contentment. Even his scars from sadistic overlords seemed shrouded beneath the radiant glow.

"Some say I am a soothsayer; others call me a thief and liar," he greeted the approaching youth. "But avoid me. Only children stop and stare and conjure thoughts of my apparent wickedness, for none of them can conceive of peace behind this mask of horror. But as *you* look at me I sense my being; a mirror reflecting the deepest fear of all your thoughts."

Rolind sat staring at the strange man, then broke the

bread in half and offered him some. The creature accepted the gift with a grin.

"Of what do you speak, old man?"

"Of you, my lord. And your fears of pain."

"What do you know of my thoughts and why do you address me as your lord?"

"Your costume is but a mask. Your skin is that of royal birth."

Rolind stared at the man's calloused stumps, then into the glassy eyes which could see nothing but the night.

"How would you know who I might be? After all, you're blind."

"Only in the eye, my lord. Only in the eye . . ."

Rolind peered coldly at the little man. "Perhaps I am a low lord's servant boy."

"Perhaps . . . but you are Rolind and you carry passages of the Book of Orange in your tears."

"You speak nonsense!"

"Your eyes reveal it true."

Rolind wished to respond but could find no words denying it.

". . . but your wanderings reveal the search for peace."

Rolind bit into the loaf of crusty bread, peering at the deformed creature before him, then drank some wine.

"Perhaps I *am* Rolind, but my tears have long since fled," he boldly declared.

"You speak of course about the diary."

Rolind quickly searched for the book, feeling it still secure against his hip.

"You believe it shall bring you peace," the cripple continued in a calm manner, "but in truth, none will hear you. Mark my words, my lord, none will hear you."

Rolind rose abruptly, shouting down at his tormentor. "You say this only because you're horribly deformed, wishing to see others suffer as you most obviously do."

"I have no suffering, sire. If I do, could it be possible to present such calmness in my speech?"

Rolind stopped at the thought and, though still angered, sat back down before the odd one.

"Listen to me then as a soothsayer instead of a monster . . . ," and with waving hands to enliven his words he began:

"There is told of a land once cast far away from here, ringed by stormy walls so high that shadows could not grow to meet their base. And in this land stand three earthen mounds, widely separated and reached by different routes. Each one offers up a different prize. One contains a thousand clocks made by men who wish perfection for the lives of other men. In another, a thousand candles made by men searching out universal truth. These two mounds are guarded by demons and great winds, but are not too difficult to reach."

"And what of the third?" came the curious voice.

"Within its mold there grows a solitary flower, created by no man and having no purpose for any man, and yet it truly is the most precious."

"How can something valueless be precious? Besides, a thousand flowers already grow within the gardens of a great many men. What need they of one?"

"Were you to find those who know of these treasures you would find the answer."

Rolind issued a quick, mocking laugh at the man's odd words. But the soothsayer stared back with greatest confidence. Rolind grew afraid and defiant.

"Then tell me where to find these men! I wish to speak to them!"

"Oftentimes you pass them in the streets, yet they will never reveal themselves, though easily distinguished from other men. Those who know the clocks are bitter towards the world, for they realize how little time exists in life and never shall they know of peace. Those who know the candles are always drowned in speech, for they must question everything around. But those who know the essence of the flower are the most difficult to recognize, for they are quiet, revealing to the universe the greatest inner peace. Yet one must be cautious in knowing them, for they are often mistaken for the dull and commonest among men."

"And this flower," the interested youth questioned, "shall I one day be in posession of it?"

"Possession? No. It is not like gold to be collected and owned. It is like an essence which shall consume you."

Rolind sat, quietly contemplating the old man's words. But unable to find any meaning in them, he shouted, "I don't understand anything you said! But I do know that the diary I carry will quickly bring me peace!"

"Hurry then," the crippled man continued in a mocking way. "For your castle lies so empty there without you, and you will miss the death. But mark my words, young prince, none shall hear you, sire. None shall hear your words."

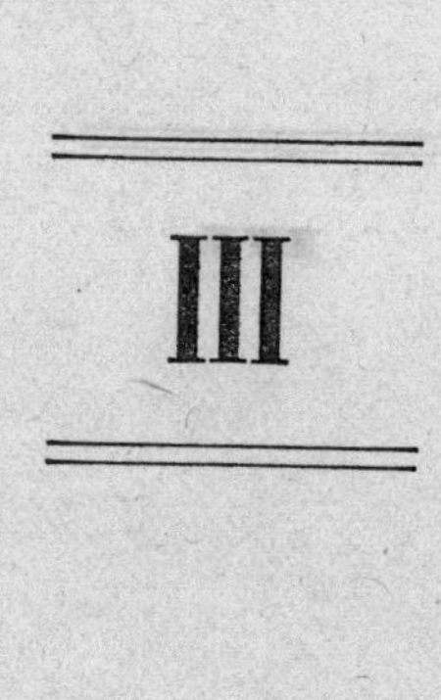

i

THE KING OF MERU, a tall lean man who wore his moustache triangular and straight, resided over the public court in a spacious chamber. Huge timbers crossed the high wide ceiling, and large hanging banners of the fifteen tribes within the realm enlivened its dark wooden walls.

At the head of the chamber, about ten feet from the wall, stood the throne, a simple structure of slated mahogany which had been molded into a comfortable seat: its two arching armrests and round curved legs made the imperial seat appear like a figure eight cut across its head and base. At the sides of the king's throne stood two similar seats for Rolind and Dels. To the king's left stood Caji, chief of the eight-foot imperial guards and beyond him, along the south wall and more in line with the ruler's sight sat four men dressed in loose-fitting shimmering orange satin vests bordered with high white ruffled collars. Upon their heads appeared soft creased bonnets made of red velveteen. These were the councillors who sat in aid to the king and had been chosen by decree of the fifteen tribes. Rolind stood hidden in the darkness of the postern behind the throne, surveying the scene.

A ragged man now stood before King Riis, accompanied by a member of the public guard. As the ruler slid his leopard cape to one side, the golden locket swung across his chest.

"Why do you waste my time with such a man? The magistrates have judged him fairly." Then turning to the guilty man, he said, "What other punishment should be your right? Your victim's life at bay, a dagger in your hand, threatening an ancient man for gold! And already you bear a mark of guilt upon your forehead and missing stumps where fingers once adorned. Six times you've stolen now. You deserve no arms! The law is the law!"

"And is the law the law when you anoint your sons in blood?" the guilty man shouted.

"How dare you!" The king rose before the hushed audience, fury raging in his eye. "Quickly cast this one to his doom, and heat the sword with oil that it may scar whatever tranquility his wretched mind may know!"

And as Rolind watched his father's anger seethe, his childish fingers felt the width of the ancient diary. He hoped his father would read its words.

The king cast his eyes to the marble floor; then as he lifted up again his lips bore a smile. "And now, what manner of man does approach?" King Riis rubbed his short black beard and quickly sat back, watching the delicate form approach; and a most unusual man it was, frail as a child dressed in green satin. As he passed along the aisle he cowered at the sight of curious eyes.

"I bring you a song, sire," the pixie squeaked.

"I see you tote a mandolin as well."

"It is my trade, sire."

"As you know, a fine song shall be rewarded with feasting."

"Sire, I bring a song from a land so far away that my master's crew had to cut new timbers for its masts, the sea-winds so corrosive that men shuddered at the thought of climbing rope for fear of its burning."

"And did this windy brine also affect your voice-strings, good man?"

"This song is meant only for the ears of our two beloved princes, sire."

The king spread his arms, indicating the empty seats on either side of him. The audience of fifty laughed.

"Perhaps, songster, if you begin this melody the two benefactors of your entertainment will appear."

The small figure blushed and smiled; then raising up the mandolin across his chest, he played upon the high notes with his voice flowing above their range.

There is told of a sea so wild
that no wind doth dare touch
for fear that the boiling waves
will turn it into dust.

There is told of a land so mountainous
that no cloud dare to scrape
for fear the pointed peaks
may puncture and deflate.

There is told of a treasure so rare
that the diamond dare not gleam
for fear the radiant glow
would turn it into steam.

There is told of a flower so precious
that a search that never ends
and the tale of a youthful pirate
who comes from many lands.

Suddenly the troubadour stopped and, bowing before the king, prepared to accept his reward. But a voice emerged from behind the throne and Rolind stepped out to take his seat.

"Your song ends too quickly," the prince anxiously spoke up, recalling the crippled soothsayer's words, reaching up to feel the crest of Byui against his chest. "Please, continue, troubadour."

"Young sire, what do you mean?" came the nervous reply.

"Every song has a sense, this one ends too soon. I have heard the beginning, now I wish to know the end."

The gaily dressed man blushed and bowing slowly, spoke, "Yes, sire," and he continued with his song.

There is told of a tear so round
as to fill the air with death
and cause the starry night
to chill a child's breath.

There is told of a scheme so bold
as to make your blood freeze cold
and make the oldest man
afraid of growing old.

But! There is also told of a heart which groans
which falseness dare not know

for fear its time in life be short
and its children never grow.

But when the moon doth lay to bed
and children's hearts do glow
there shall be sown an earthly place
where the dreams of men can grow.

And upon this soil the seed shall spring
and flowers blossom full
and into all men's lives shall come
the peaceful kingdom's rule.

These things I sing to you
speak of present dreams
but also of a latter-day
filled with happy scenes.

For though our sorrow sings today
and echoes through our land
the sun shall always warm again
the coldest, oldest man.

"From what land do these words come?" Rolind quickly begged.

"A land far from here where the seas crash loud with fury. We came upon a man floundering upon a great raft. And a strange scene it was, for the weather seemed not too overbearing for such an elderly life, yet we became fearful of our own. But he showed no fear and when we laid aside to offer aid, this bearded ancient sang with a voice as gentle as a bird, and put my *own* art to shame."

"Where is this land and who is this man?" demanded the curious youth.

"I don't know, young sire. I am but a songster. My captain is our navigator."

"Then tell me who your captain is, so that I might quiz him too."

"Lermo, sire. Captain Lermo."

The noisy chamber suddenly drew still: the shuffling feet and the echo-whispering ceased as the king arose to shout, "Lermo! That thief and pirate! How dare you bring this man's presence here with you?"

"A pirate, my lord? His reputation cannot be so rewarding as that. It is true that he is feared among men, but beneath his calloused skin a gentleness lies which could turn the bleakest day into a priceless jewel. His reputation has been earned because he trades among the western lands; there all men are rough and only the toughest can survive. One should not judge him by those who malign, but by those who praise."

"But it is said that he would plunder without fear, and has cast a hundred to their death. Even his name brings fear to *me!*"

"Oh, my lord . . . such are mere tales sown by those who bemoan their own dull lives and would fear to brave real perils. I can attest that this man Lermo has never pilfered any treasure, and those who have died by his hand dared foolishly to raise the first sword. His wealth has been earned, great sire, and his chest is filled with honest gold."

"You, yourself, allude quite often to wealth. Is such your only dream?"

"I am confused, my king. Can you believe such words after hearing my art? If it were true, then I should woddle as a suckling pig. And yet, whilst it is true that I would hesitate before the offering of any ruby or sapphire, never would I toss away these strings for wealth, and neither would my captain. His scars and his laughter have never been for trade."

"Would he not rob my ships if they were laden with gold and spice?" the king asked in a more relaxed voice, obviously impressed by the man's presentation. Even Rolind stared with interest at the novel description of this most-feared man.

"No man's ship would he rob, sire, lest they turn upon him first. But have no fear, my king, for Lermo is a most loyal servant of imperial rule. In fact, he bade I give the prince this." He turned to face Rolind and withdrew from a purse a dark-stained hardwood box covered with deep round knots, delicately soft, truly a master's work.

"Why is this for me and not for my brother?" Rolind begged, afraid.

"For he does not sit here today, sire . . ." the troubadour said, pointing towards the empty throne.

With an embarrassed smile and amidst the laughter of the audience, Rolind accepted the box. As he did, Dels entered unnoticed and sat upon his throne. But Rolind continued undisturbed, looking within the box, staring at the gift within: a red-petaled flower resting on a bed of yellow velvet. Though without roots, this flower pulsated with the awesome appearance of a beckoning dance. Rolind quickly closed the lid, and stared deeply into the little man's eyes. "Tell me quick . . . where did you pluck this?"

"Pluck sire? Why we plucked nothing. The old sage of the raft begifted this plant to us. He claimed its petals cast tranquility for those who care to dream. Look back into its beauty and I shall sing you its song."

Rolind responded to the request, staring deeply at the pulsating form:

My petals are red
they pulsate with life:

in my face you shall see a clock
that ticks away the hours,
and from my fragrance you shall be enhanced
by the odors of nymphs and bowers.

And when the candles are all aglow,
and the moon shall make an hour,
my rhythm shall give you eternal peace
within my earthen tower.

Hear no man I say!

A word is a will,
a promise, a lie,
but a dream is a field of flowers.

You shall dream I say
of a magical day
when beauty shall be your power:

the cry, the tear, the pain, the fear,
shall all be turned to stone;

the laugh, the grin, the smile . . .
shall take a while,
but will grow within your home.

Youth is my age,
song is my way,
stare into my dance and evil shall melt away.

Roland looked up, startled by the jester's words.

"Enough of this!" shouted the king, standing up and pointing at the troubadour. "You are a most disturbing imp!"

"Let the man sing!" came a soft, but defiant voice deep within the public audience. All eyes turned upon the stranger as he arose.

Rolind also turned toward the defiant voice, shocked at recognizing the *Li Scholar* from the Gazebah.

King Riis continued to shout, but this time directing his voice towards the white-clothed ancient who stood within the crowd.

"How dare you interfere with these matters! You are only a *Li Scholar* and have no say in regal ways!" he shouted, staring wide-eyed and angered at the man.

"This jester's song fills your mind with punishment, for you know what truth lies within his words."

"You have no voice in these matters!" King Riis snapped at the soft-spoken man.

"Every citizen has a voice when it is known that one prince must die at the hand of another. Once this kingdom served for all men, and the king no more important than any other, but . . ."

"I do not need a lesson in history!"

". . . but you have taken it upon yourself to create a situation which violates basic principles of the *Li.* You refuse to allow your sons' natures to rule their lives."

The king suddenly looked away into the eyes of his subjects who turned back to face him.

"And what makes you believe that I have any such

plan?" he stuttered, attempting to appease the crowd before him. But the *Li Scholar* spoke on.

"When your troops drove hard upon those in the Gazebah for merely acting out innocent history written in the Book of Orange, you aroused suspicion, and many read the passage with keener curiosity."

"Out! You speak nonsense!"

The eight-foot soldiers approached the *Li Scholar* just as Rolind rose to speak his mind. But he was overwhelmed by shock as he watched the royal guards push their way between the aisles and subdue the ancient man. Others in the chamber turned and quickly fled. The old voice called out above the crowd, "You may eject me now, but when your son's blood spills into your eye, the power of this kingdom shall weaken and the enemies of our tranquil manner will rise and destroy forever the peace once created within the land of Fre."

"Guards! Cast him out! There is no voice in these matters but royal decree!"

And as the old man was rudely handled by the powerful guards, his last few words echoed aloud for all to hear. "It is the royal mind which casts the mask of death upon this land . . . and will cause its great destruction!"

"Father . . ."

"There is no need for words, Rolind!" the angry king said to his son.

"But I carry proof of your error . . . ," he said, withdrawing the diary for the man to see.

"I will not discuss it any more!"

"But, Father . . ."

The king cast a furious eye towards his son, holding back his raging anger. But Rolind raised an accusing finger towards the man.

"It is you! You have made this madness reality! You have forced the people in this realm to believe those words written over two hundred years ago, words which I can prove are false!"

"I will not discuss the matter with you!"

"You have simply tried to justify it all with nonsense logic! It isn't fair to me or Dels! You condemn your sons to die because of your view of the mystical past!"

The king remained angry at his bitter son, while Rolind turned to face his brother, Dels. For a moment he stared into defeat, then quickly turned his attention to the throne. His father turned away.

"Oh, Father. Dels will not protest, but I must!" He waved the book for all to see. "These beliefs of yours are wrong and yet you refuse to look at words I carry here as proof. Oh, how you have destroyed everything which might be beautiful in life: games cannot be played without a fight, nor dare we receive gifts, nor even listen to a song without the constant reminder that you have conceived a future filled with doom! Is there no other perception in this universe but your own single truth?"

"Rolind, listen . . ." King Riis reached out to subdue his son.

"No! Never again. I carry proof of your error, but such insolence to this *Li Scholar* makes me shudder at your narrowness of mind!"

And with those words Rolind turned, blinded with tears to all those eyes on him, and quickly fled the throne. And as he ran he held dearly in his grip the ancient book and Captain Lermo's mystical gift.

ii

WALLS AND CORRDOR FLOORS appeared distorted behind the prism flood of tears. Somewhere in the universe existed peace, but Rolind knew not where. His mind raced confused. As he reached his room, he thrust himself upon the bed, and cried in mindless fit, seeking comprehension for his adolescent mind. Oh, how he wished to understand his father's apparent madness and the motives of the others in his life. And though he moaned and moaned, no answers came.

As the tears finally ceased and his muffled whimper permitted him a chance to hear, there came the scratchy shadow of the soothsayer's voice:

None shall hear you . . . None shall hear you . . .

And he sought to touch the diary and find comfort in its words. But his eyes teared again and the haunting words echoed in his cars:

None shall hear you . . . None shall hear you . . . None shall hear you.

Rolind turned to see beyond the open obiel. Seagulls passed him by, a fluffy cloud hung on high. Then slowly he rose and entered the rounded cage, peering out to follow the length of apron of the distant palisade.

On your return I shall be there to greet you . . . It is half yours for sleep . . . here, to keep you warm . . . Then looking down towards the wharfs . . . Oh, how wonderful it would be if Polin were still there.

Though still wearing the royal locket and his regal garb, Rolind hurried from the room, racing down the corridors, down to the lowest levels of the castle, back to his secret passageway. And as effortlessly as before, he shimmied through the rock-lined orifice, sealing in the darkness all around. As he reached the final turn, his mind became a blur of confusion; his heartbeat stopped.

A flicker of candlelight! Rolind could hardly believe his eyes. Never before had he seen such flame within the maze unless it was he who carried the wick. Fear tightened up his gut. Cautiously, he moved forward, anxious of what next he might see, and stepped into the well-lit room: boulders black with dust, dancing flames cast shadows upon the rounded rock. And there before his sacred exit stood two giant royal guards, with steel-armored cups protruding from thick leather bands across bright red shirts, each holding a five-foot spiked shield to protect their massive frames. Two spears crossed near the base, blocking his path. Their stare was cold and stoic. Rolind slowly approached.

"Move aside!" he shouted out, standing before the shields. But neither guard responded to his words.

"Stand aside!" he commanded more defiantly. "I am your prince! Stand aside!" But the soldiers stood in silent vigilance; and as fear and anger overwhelmed the boy, he rushed forward, shouting and beating bare fists against the heavy plates.

"Stand aside! Stand aside! Stand aside!" He battered them until his hands burnt red with pain. And soon his words were muffled by his tears. The youth stepped back, staring directly in their eyes.

"Please," he begged. "You don't understand what is happening." And then shouting again: "You have no reason to hinder my freedom! Stand aside!"

A cold hand touched his skin, and made him jump. Then a voice gently said, "Come with me."

Rolind turned and stared.

"You will find no peace here." Tyre then spoke again and turned his ward around, away from the candlelight. He led the youth back into the darkness of the maze.

"Tyre, make them part and set me free."

The kindly mentor continued with his push and proclaimed, "Only the king can order them."

"Then help me advise some other escape." No answer came and the mentor continued to lead his ward through the darkness.

"You realize that this path leads me to death."

"Come . . . Your father has requested an audience. You must speak with him, not me." Tyre's voice remained emotionless and Rolind peered up, unable to see his mentor's face.

"But he will never listen!" Rolind protested, and he twisted to be free.

"And I am powerless to help . . ."

The path along which Tyre led Rolind seemed a strange one to the prince, but in his confused state and within the blackness of the space, Rolind could not determine his position within the maze. The path was endless and Rolind begged for a pardon from his fate.

"Tell me, Tyre, what has your part been in all of this?"

First the old man hesitated, then retorted in a gentle tone, "Do you not understand the role of a guardian-teacher?"

"Of course; to aid the prince in becoming king."

Tyre remained silent.

"So . . . you taught me history, culture, politics . . . and," Rolind snapped, "the dagger." He stopped their advance and turned to face the distant face.

"Has that always been the guardian-teacher's role, or just recently upon the request of my father?"

"Your question does not apply at this moment," Tyre calmly answered, continuing to prod the boy along. But Rolind refused to move.

"How dare you become deceitful when now you serve the king and not the prince! Once you taught me when all elements of time are blended into one they make a beauty in the universe. Why did you lie?"

"I have had only one role and that has been to groom you for the throne."

"Even if it destroys my sanity?" the prince shouted out. And in a bitter tone he demanded, "Does Gytre offer Dels this very argument?"

"As you know, I have no knowledge of any mind besides my own."

"You lie!"

Tyre remained silent, and as Rolind felt defenseless in the maze, he gave up his arguments and followed behind the prodding grip. Where they stopped, Tyre pushed against a boulder, rotating it on a hinge, and allowed the castle light to flood in Rolind's eyes. The two stepped out.

As his sight returned, Rolind knew the spot—a portion of the hall just beside the public chamber. An anger grew, then quickly died as he looked in Tyre's eyes. His stomach tightened and a drop of urine formed.

"I fear my father!" he shouted to the white-haired man.

"You shall have to deal with him on your own terms. I cannot act in defiance of my role."

"But you *did* interfere with my future!"

"There is no way in which I can interfere with your *Li*." Tyre stood staring back into Rolind's eyes. And as the youth realized the futility of debate, he allowed himself to be led into a small chamber alongside the secret passageway.

THERE HE SAT BY DELS, not daring to look up or speak for fear that words would release his most sensitive feelings. The young prince nervously followed the contours of grain within the dark wood, moving his fingers up towards the goblet of wine which stood before his place.

"Perhaps Father will read the diary," he fantasized to himself. "Then all will be solved."

Tyre gently touched his shoulder. But as Rolind looked up to speak, King Riis entered the room, his six-foot stature slumping as he crossed the space. Though tears were obvious, Rolind believed them false.

"These drinks are here for you—a special brew, a liquor made of many grapes with fruit enough for taste."

Rolind hesitated, his hand just below the goblet stem. "Father, will you read the diary that I brought?"

"Now, drink this wine, it will make you more at ease and we can talk."

"There is nervousness in your speech, Father. Why did you seal off the castle?"

"Drink. Then tell me where the diary lies."

Excitement filled Rolind's brain and he conjured thoughts of victory. And in this momentary glee, he brought the thick, red liquor to his lips.

"Then you will read it?"

"Yes . . ."

Rolind drank most deeply.

"It lies upon my bed. Read it now, Father, please."

"And the wine?"

"A fine flavor which dries my eyes."

Then his father turned and as the door shut behind the men, Rolind looked up to Tyre. The white-haired mentor prompted him to rise as Gytre led Dels out the other side.

"Come, Rolind." Tyre's voice spoke softly, his touch gentle.

"I feel strange, Tyre, a bit light, yet strong enough to stand."

The mentor led him out along the corridors to the stairway, then down.

"Why this way, Tyre?"

The old man remained silent. Rolind looked up, afraid of what words might fill the air.

"I feel uneasy, Tyre."

"There is nothing to fear," he said, still leading the boy with hands across narrow shoulders.

"Do you lead me to my death?" the youth questioned meekly.

But Tyre remained silent, leading the prince down to the lowest level of the castle where the dust of centuries clung to moist, cold walls, and where only candles lit the way. He led the youth into a small dark cubicle. Rolind stared at a solitary candle, its form a blur of yellow light.

"I feel weak, Tyre, almost without will. Has father drugged me?"

Tyre sat him upon a small wooden stool.

"I feel no capacity to protest nor even to fear, yet I wish to escape. I beg you, Tyre . . ."

"Here," the mentor said, exposing a black silk loincloth. "You must wear only this. There is no need to protest."

"But I *have* need," he begged while Tyre began undressing him. "Father said he would read the diary, therefore no reason exists for this."

"We must wait until he returns . . . there . . . does the dampness chill your skin?"

"It is the fear which chills my mind," the sickened youth pleaded, but Tyre led him, hand in hand, beyond the room and through a blackened dusty passageway. The cold creased Rolind's skin and his brain now ached with pain.

iv

As they emerged from the passageway Rolind looked up to see long fingers of candlelight dancing feverishly upon large gray boulders, with blackness high above them. Then catching sight of Dels' approach with Gytre by his side, he stopped to face the other. He explored Dels' bare chest and stoic face. Then without warning Tyre placed a cold object in his grip, forcing him to look upon the ancient dagger of Fre. He searched his brother's eyes and begged conciliation, but Dels' remained a stoic face. Fear overwhelmed the youth as he saw a similar weapon in his brother's hand. Rolind turned to question Tyre, but the guardian-teacher no longer stood beside him.

A voice commanded from above, "You must strike each other!"

Rolind looked up to see his father's face, half-hidden in the gallery above.

"I feel weak, Father. Have you not read the diary?"

"You must strike each other," came the unemotional voice.

Rolind's head dropped weakly through his grip on the weapon grew strong. Too weak for words, the prince stared into his brother's eyes. His arms felt limp, yet the dagger pointed up.

Suddenly Dels' arm shot forward and Rolind stared at the dagger tip only inches from his chest. Quickly he searched his brother's face for reason, but found nothing save his stoic stare.

"Don't lose control, dear brother. It is all a game. If we wish, our feet could dance all day and our hands be used for art. It is only a drug, not desire which makes you aim your weapon at my heart." As Dels' head dropped, strength returned to Rolind's arms, as though the threat had suddenly awakened him. The dagger rested easily in his grip.

Suddenly Dels raised the dagger tip again, this time lunging hard towards Rolind's heart. The prince leapt back, staring at the orange candlelight reflecting off the blade. Then he looked up to watch sweat bead across Dels' smooth forehead. He opened out his palm to plead for peace.

But Dels hurled himself again, thrusting the dagger point towards his brother's eyes. Rolind instinctively parried the attack with an open arm, grabbing Dels around the back and forcing him down against the dusty rock. The beleaguered Dels twisted violently as Rolind held him, rolling with his frenzied twin, avoiding the blade. Finally he pressed the attacking arm firmly against the floor. Rolind's muscles ached and his face twisted in the struggle. And as he stared into Dels' frenzied face, he saw a silent but wretched scream of rage, great torment pouring from his brother's mouth. Dust flew up to blind the youth and caused him to struggle even more intently against the blindness in his eye, trying to subdue the swinging arms around him. Suddenly Dels' power drained and the twirling momentum threw Rolind off his brother's chest.

Quickly Rolind looked up . . . the attack had stopped. Rolind slowly rose, wiping the stinging particles of sand from his legs and face. His lungs breathed deep, his temples throbbed strenuously. But his eyes, transfixed upon Dels' own stare, watched an uncontrollable flow of tears and the nodding head which seemed to communicate a similar state of disbelief.

Yet no sooner was he relaxed when Dels swung his dagger round, drawing a cold line across the brother's chest. The sharp sensation quickly vanished, leaving Rolind both expressionless and unconcerned. His stare was of disbelief. A trickle of blood streaked down his belly, and his eyes opened wide, wanting to scream out across the space and stop this insanity.

But Dels leapt forward again, lunging the blade tip towards Rolind's chest, and no longer could the youth behave defensively. Instead his own moves became sure and quick, parrying each attack so as to draw his brother close and end the fight.

The cold arena wall pressed hard against his skin. No longer could the youth retreat. His gaze remained transfixed, his attention on his brother's form. He became devoid of moral thought, no longer was he an intelligent creature, he had become a cornered beast displaying only one instinct—to survive! All conscious senses focused on the threat ahead, his strength enhanced with every breath. Even the flickering candlelight no longer interfered with his sight, nor did questions of absurdity muddle his mind. He was now the beast relieved of all those human fears.

At the next attack Rolind beat Dels' arm away, then lunged, screaming out, forcing his brother's head back and raising up his own dagger for Dels to see. But the other repositioned himself for still another strike.

Now the drug's full effect played on Rolind's mind: agression became genuine and drove him forward to strike Dels' arm and to attack with slow, sure strikes of his own. His eyes dilated, his breaths came short and quick, answering the other's attacks with a parry, then a slash. Dels struck and Rolind parried, bringing the weapon back quickly and slashing Dels' forearm, knocking the weapon from his hand. Quickly the prince lunged and with all the fury which his body stored, and blinded by the rage, leapt forward towards his brother's heaving chest; driving the blade hard to find the mark to cut a moist warm wound. Then suddenly his consciousness returned again. He watched the wreath of cataclysmic pain draw across his brother's face, and heard that bleat, a final gasp for air. And his own mind shouted out its words for Dels to hear: apologies, denial of the fact. Cheek to cheek he pressed against Dels' skin, and begged for love as he loosened his grip on the blade, and cried so pitifully into the corpse's ear, hugging his most lifeless form that lay there as a whimpering child must do, swathed in a blood-drenched death.

i

ROLIND AWOKE, barely able to raise his lids. The pungent odor of alum and dried blood suffused the air. And though he strained to see, he fell back into a torturous swirl, wrestling hysterically with the phantom weapon in his hand. Again and again he swung his limp arms, repositioning that deadly blade, lunging over and over again, desperately in search of that *exact* moment when the tip first pierced the flesh, struggling to withdraw the dagger just in time. But, with each lunge did he feel it rip the naked skin. And again he drew back his hand, trying to find a way to avoid that final strike, wanting to stop, wanting to end the torment in his mind.

ii

Again the troubled youth awoke. A solitary candle lit the darkness and the gentle sound of harp strings filled the air. Rolind ran his hand across the crust of flaked alum upon his wound, then reached up to stroke his smooth black hair.

"My lord . . ." A deep voice interrupted his stillness, a humble sound, yet demanding of his mind. The flickering candle shadowed the speaker's face, and the harp music ceased to sound.

"Caji?" Rolind weakly looked up. "Why does the king's own guard stand before *me?*"

The giant remained at attention, and Rolind conjured up the words, "The king is dead." Tears flowed freely and the thick, sweet liquid settled on his tongue. A warm, gentle hand stroked his brow.

"Oh, Tyre," Rolind searched around, pleading. "It is madness, or do I dream?"

"There is great strength within your *Li.*"

"But never did I seek this *Li.* Never did I choose it as a farmer might. It was thrust upon me like a knife!" His screaming filled the room and within each sigh recurred the final cry of Dels.

"Your tears will dry."

As Rolind looked up, his eyes swelled with bitterness. "Dels is dead by my father's plan, and now I am king by my father's hand. Is it true, Tyre?"

"It is true, Rolind. You are king."

Rolind found no more tears but slowly turned his attention towards the imperial guard.

Caji stepped forward.

"Sire, Meru is under seige. Five hundred Kinu tribesmen have landed near Sessu below the eastern palisade.

They bear the crest of Byui. The ouster of the *Li Scholar* has caused great commotion and many swords have clashed."

Rolind stared back into the starlight, bemoaning his own fate and Callio's rashness. Then he announced a royal decree.

"Sound the death knell. News of King Riis's death will make them moan. Send couriers into the streets, Caji. Spread the news quickly. There exists no need for blood."

Caji turned to leave.

"And fetch the man called Callio. Present him with my crest. He will gladly come."

As the guard left, Rolind tried to turn away and cry. But a powerful presence disturbed his wish for grief, and the boy-king looked up to face his mentor.

"Shall I leave you now? My role to serve ends now that you are king."

"No, Tyre! I fear the night and seek some comfort."

"And tomorrow?"

"No! I cannot remain alone. Aid me as my counsel, please."

"As you wish. I shall refuse to leave until your mind knows true happiness and ease."

Then stroking the boy's sweat-dried hair, Tyre quietly returned to strum the highest tones upon the harp.

THAT NIGHT HELD TERROR for the boy-king. To his sleep came constant memories of his brother's death. And when the sunlight rudely awoke the youth, his bed lay soaked with sweat. No harp songs rang and the morning sounds were a muffled lull. Rolind rose up in a daze but quickly reached out to the bookshelf and, locating Lermo's magic gift, opened up the lid to stare at the pulsating petals within. Then he donned the green gabardine slacks, and with the box securely in his grip, glided along the castle corridors and down into the public chamber, holding back the haunting images which lay within his mind. Once behind the throne he stopped before a door near the councillor's place and, passing through, descended to the crypt below. Moisture pained his wound and his brain reeled, still weakened by the loss of blood.

The vault into which he entered was but a narrow corridor; marble slabs emerged from smooth black obsidian walls. Here before him, candles lit the remains of all those kings since Byui, all dressed in regal clothes long faded and dull with dust.

First he stopped before the corpse of Awio draped in eons of decay, its bony sockets wide as if the eyes could stare out beyond the hollowness of death. Rolind's anger swelled for he knew this corpse to be a fraud and quickly fled away. Rows of corpses loomed, each skull covered with blackened skin and stringy hair.

Tall orange candles at the distant end flickered near the corpses of Riis and Dels. Rolind surveyed their quiet forms draped in bright red velvet capes bordered wide with soft white fur. Each bore the smooth golden crest of Byui across the chest. Rolind stared bitterly at his father's face, cursing the man with a deep, muffled growl.

Then he stepped away to stand by Dels and peer into those lifeless eyes. The face rested still, bulging, swollen, its skin like wet sand; its lips and cheeks twisted by a taunting grin. Rolind surveyed the corpse—a statue, so it seemed, filling up his mind with realization that this had once been a living boy.

As he knelt down, leaning across the lifeless chest, he reached out to touch the face. And though afraid his touch might disturb its sleep, Rolind gently drew tender fingers across the cheeks. He whispered:

"Please, Dels. I love you so. Please don't burden me with blame."

As he touched the chin he reached down to open the wooden box, and placed the pulsating flower atop the crest of Byui. He stared into the dancing petals, visualizing Dels and himself at play, skipping madly about, gyrating and laughing, throwing pebbles off the castle roof: happy, carefree, peaceful . . . and alive.

iv

HOURS PASSED and Rolind awoke, gazing back at Dels's face. Then he rose and retreated past the gallery of death, ascending through the square orifice. As he emerged into the royal chamber Caji stood beside the throne.

"Has Lermo been found?"

"Sire?" the confused guard began. "I know nothing of this man, Lermo. But we have found Callio and he now awaits your presence."

"Oh," he said, realizing his error. "Call the council. I shall presently appear."

As the guard turned to carry out the king's command, Rolind called him back again.

"Caji! Wait! I wish you to seek out a sea-trader called Lermo. Perhaps his vessel still lies along the harbor shore. It is with urgency your messengers must go. And should he hesitate, implore the man to come. I have great need of him."

V

To reach the Council Room, Rolind passed through a postern lying to the right of the throne. His pace was swift, although great pain throbbed across his wound. As he entered the chamber and stood within the obiel, he stared out across the harbor down below, surveying the busy scene, searching across the waters, hoping to spot a vessel which might be Lermo's ship. But the moments passed by quickly and the boy-king turned to face the banner-covered walls around the room. Fifteen flags hung before his eyes, and he surveyed each one. Then he approached a cupboard to his left and, carefully withdrawing four silver goblets and a golden chalice, placed them upon the dark oak five-cornered table at the center of the room. Within each he carefully poured red wine from the already filled decanter near his throne, and when he had completed the chore, sat upon his throne. The youth felt nauseated; his head drooped to the side. But a sudden noise from the corridor urged him to sit erect and greet each entering councillor with a nod.

The four men quickly entered and took their seats. They sat solemn and quiet. Only Eti did Rolind see; his bald, rounded head and fat fingers supporting a flabby chin; haunting, peering eyes.

Then Caji led Callio in, and quickly positioned himself beside the door. The Kinu tribesman stood quietly at first, surveying the room. Then as his eyes met the king's, he pointed a finger and stared wide-eyed.

"It's you! The boy . . . Our king? Oh, sire, if it is revenge you seek, I accept all punishment."

"No! Only do I beg you withdraw your men and return to the Bintu frontier. As you see, the family of Byui still reigns, but your loyalty and vigilance must be as strong."

"My pledge still stands the same, sire. It is the kingdom which we serve."

"Enough! I thank you for your love, Callio. Now go. These are perilous times. Our enemy may find us easy to destroy unless we stand as one."

Callio stared into the young king's eyes, a smile overcoming his strong, gaunt features. "Thank you, sire. We shall return home at once, and forever recall your grace." Then he bowed and left.

Rolind tightly closed his eyes, bringing the golden chalice to his lips. He sucked the liquid, preparing for a councillor's speech, carefully avoiding Eli's cold, observing glare.

"How do you know this man, Callio, sire?" a high-pitched voice inquired.

"Surely you speak in jest, Vernon, for it has been your knowledge all along of my departures from the castle."

"Departures from the castle?" The white-haired councillor quickly arose. "Had we ever suspected such departures, surely we would have seen an early end to them."

"There is no more need to jest. My father knew and you advised him seal the castle in order to force my hand in slaying Dels."

"No, sire. This idea is new to us." He spoke to agreeing nods from the other men. "Too much fear of the Bintu exists within us to have tolerated any departure of the prince. Never before has any other left the sanctuary of this fortress without adequate protection along the way. Tell us, sire, where this exit lies and we shall forever secure our sovereigns' safety."

Rolind stood up. "Enough! Enough of your games!"

"The safety of our monarch is our only concern," the councillor insisted.

Rolind turned away, not wishing to speak with the man. But Vernon continued after a momentary pause:

"Does the king trust Callio with pleasure when it is the Kinu who trades with the Bintu? They know the king is new and such a siege could be nothing save a trick preceding invasion."

Rolind quickly looked up, angered by the councillor's words.

"How dare you accuse a man who has suffered so grievously my woe . . ."

"We know not of that. But we know our tribes demand protection against the Bintu menace."

"I have concerns of my own! For within my mind I suffer from the callous actions of those around me!"

"Lest you forget!" Vernon cut into Rolind's speech, "It is these ogres to the south who each year seize a hundred youths your very age to castrate and lash to trees near our homes."

Rolind turned away.

"And do not believe my concern is hollow when once it was my own son whom I had to find this way and watch him die before my eyes!"

Rolind turned back sharply. "I do not like these words of pain!"

"And we cannot afford to have you weakened when the Bintu plot our death. They have stood beyond our borders for three hundred years now—ever since the ancient kings made battle for this throne."

"The Bintu! The Bintu! How dare you speak of other things when you stand before this grieving youth?"

Vernon challenged Rolind's stare.

"You speak of Callio and plots, yet did it ever cross your mind to see the scheme to murder Dels was cruel enough to be a Bintu way?"

The councillor faltered in his speech and, without words to speak, weakly sat back down. Rolind continued with his thoughts.

"Tell me, Vernon, who fixed the drug for Dels and me? Could not such diversion be treated as murder? After all, most Tsiu tribesmen are physicians, learned in herbs and medicines. Should I not punish Tsiu, and yourself a member?"

"It is of Callio we spoke, not . . ."

"If Callio is guilty of treason, whom do we accuse of murder?!"

Vernon looked away.

"At night I dreamt of murder, Vernon, yet peacefulness did share your dreams. And you, Jani," he turned to another, "tell me of my father's mind! Did he conceive this plot alone? Or did his eldest councillor, a Gimbu, conceive the art from his tribal sense of beauty?"

Jani looked up, startled, and released the goblet in his hand. "Sire, you torment yourself with thoughts which serve no cause. None of us here wished the act. It merely served your father's plan. When we spoke our thoughts he called us fools, afraid to see the truth." Jani looked away. "The accused, sire, is dead . . ."

"But I carried proof of his error, why did he refuse to listen? You sat there, why did you not bother him to hear? I waved the book before you all!" he cried, holding back his tears.

"*We* never saw your proof. Besides, none of us could change his mind," Jani continued in a pleading voice. "As did we disagree, so your father was convinced. But you, young sire, cannot find peace through accusations. It is finished. Now you must look upon yourself for what you are."

"And what is that? A murderer?"

"No, sire. A victim."

Rolind turned away to face the sky beyond. No birds soared high, no clouds floated by. Quietly he rose and, staring across the palisade's edge, felt an urge to climb the beckoning wall.

"Perhaps this is not my reign," he said quietly, exploring the shadows of cornfields high above. "There is too much confusion in my mind." He turned to face the others. "Awio was a fraud and my father was duped by it! Yet all those around my sire and the masses in the kingdom believed the error. I cannot accept that he alone conceived the plot! And you, Plio!" He pointed at a long-nosed councillor who suddenly looked up from his half-full goblet.

"What are your words? How do you dispel such thoughts?"

"I, sire? Do you accuse Plio of planting thoughts within your father's mind? I need no defense nor excuse, nor should you charge each tribe with disloyalty for how a Meru conceived his own fate! If treachery did exist, certainly it came from a source beyond this council!"

Rolind sat down, startled by Plio's harsh treatment of his manner.

"Yet," Plio continued in a softer tone, "I too have been concerned with your father's logic: for most certainly he loved you and truly perplexed was he by the problem. He seemed so tortured, yet no other remedy would come to mind. Most surely he must have planned to live and aid you through your grief. King Riis was not a callous man, yet his own life did he pluck, so it seems . . ."

"Are your thoughts mere diversions?" demanded Rolind.

"It does seem peculiar, sire," Vernon offered. "And this suicide. Your father's plan followed such precise logic that it burdens me to believe that he would take his own life with such emotion, and leave you without comfort in these days."

"But Tyre is my comfort!"

"Then it is by Tyre's own choosing that he stays beyond requirement. The man has fulfilled his role and must be dismissed."

"No!" Rolind shouted. "It is he who aids me now with counsel."

"And ourselves?" Plio demanded above the sudden chatter from the others. "Do we not live to serve?"

"I . . . I need him still. It is more personal than politics."

"Does Tyre become a crutch and the king admit weakness before his subjects?" Jani demanded.

"You have no right to say that!" Rolind shouted angrily.

But Vernon spoke: "The king of Meru rules fifteen tribes with the council as his guide. The guardian-teacher has no role beyond that of serving the prince's education. To change his stature would be to weaken the power of the throne."

Rolind looked nervously at this rational man, frightened by Eti's continued quiet stare.

"And tell us, from whom shall you seek council for matters of state?"

"Why, you of course!"

"Then *what* purpose does Tyre serve?"

"You confuse me! You confuse me!"

"We demand an explanation!" Jani stood up to face the raging boy.

"I shall give it when I wish!" he countered, stepping away from the throne.

"Are you not man enough to answer, sire, but seek exits from the very problem which you face?"

Rolind faced the white-haired man. "Then tell me, Vernon," he pleaded, "who is left to trust?"

"You doubt your councillors, yet have heard our case. Certainly a fifth should not rank above us. You speak of plots, sire. Tell us then how Tyre earned such a noble place amongst us? Have you asked yourself this?"

"Should I doubt he who raised me?"

"As much as any man."

Rolind looked away again. The still daylight beyond the room filled his eyes and he quietly approached the obiel. Three ships lay anchored in the bay, another crossed the dark blue waterline; the pulsating flower danced before his eyes. Then he turned and leaned against the ledge. "I find no answers here amongst you . . . I have sought out Captain Lermo as my aide."

Plio rose. "Another, sire? Is there such distrust of us?"

"You take all this too personally," Rolind pleaded. "It is peace I seek, not revenge. I need absolution from my terror. This castle only offers me continued pain."

"If it is peace you seek, sire, surely it will come with time."

"I do not want to wait!"

"And your life, sire? There is danger on the sea. Your death would serve none and bring even more pain to the subjects of your realm."

"Perhaps it is better to die than suffer during life."

Jani rose and quieted Rolind with a stare. Meekly the boy-king sat down.

"Then think of the empire, sire, and the thousands who rely on you. Without a king, truly our enemy shall find ease in our destruction. And without a prince to follow surely all our children will die."

"And who concerns himself with me! Who helped me when I held Dels' life within my grip?"

"It is over with!" Jani interrupted Rolind's rage. "Only the present and future concern us now."

"Then I shall lay the seed to bear! Will this appease you?"

"Oh, sire . . . sire. We do not seek to punish you. Our love is too great. Only do we wish to temper your youthful impetuousness. No good can come from conflict, nor even from flight. If revenge is what you seek, or eventual peace, it would be better to search it here."

"There is no need for speech, Jani," the fifteen-year-old spoke behind his grief and approached the postern: "I shall leave on Lermo's ship to seek the treasure of the storm. In *it* shall I find peace as I did beside my brother's grave. And if I suffer, then I shall be the one who makes the plan."

VI

Rolind's retreat was swift, yet long. The corridors seemed so narrow then, and the guards along the way appeared as threatening figures staring stoically past the boy. It was in his private chamber that he sought some momentary peace, yet hesitated before the entranceway. A silhouette stood before the blinding sun, long straight hair full behind the silken gown. Then the woman turned, sending smiles across the room.

"The sun is beautiful," she softly spoke and reached out to touch her son. "A testimony of joy."

"It has been long since last we stood like this," he cautiously called out across the space.

"Then come and view the sun with me."

"It hurts my eyes, and . . ." Rolind ran across the void, burying his tear-soaked eyes against her breast and she held him close, melting the sorrow deep inside. The boy relaxed beneath his mother's touch. "Is it that I must only suffer now in life and find no peace?"

The gentle woman kneeled before his eyes, holding up his chin with gentle fingertips. Rolind explored her hazel eyes.

"Why are there no tears, Mother? Have they become invisible?" he asked, touching her cheek.

"They have fled amongst the stars, Rolind dear. They are gone now."

"And the grief?" he begged.

"It can never leave, yet I shall never let it cripple me. Peace will come when treasures gleam before your eye and pain is recognized to be a temporary thing."

"But I still see the tragedy before me. The stillness of my mind echoes the terror of his scream."

"It shall vanish, dear."

"Your words come too easily, Mother." He stared off towards the distant hills.

"But they are not hollow." She drew his eyes back to hers.

Rolind sensed the meaning of her words, and then reached out to embrace this woman's neck. Countless moments filled them both with tears and strength.

"Come and play your harp," she said, leading her son across the room.

"I fear to hear my tremor in its sounds."

"Truly the music is your mind, but it can also fill your time with peace. And though each melody may end with tears, the dreams will flow as song, not scenes."

They stood before the golden instrument and Rolind reached out to touch its pillar, hearing the tones so long stilled.

"No! I fear them!" he cried and turned away. "They too know my sensitivities and would strike my ears with sorrow. It is better to let them rest, as I wish to do right now."

"Shall I bring you tea?"

"No, Mother. I desire rest. My eyes are tired. I shall cry no more, have no fear."

"Then I shall visit in the morning and sit by you," she said, and brushed his hair and left the boy upon the bed.

vii

ROLIND'S SLEEP PASSED QUICKLY and he awoke upon a pillow soaked with tears. Morning had still not broken and the boy-king arose, and in a daze traversed the long, hollow corridors to return to his brother's corpse. And there before Dels' placid stare, Rolind dreamed contentedly as though the dancing petals drew him through the air. The throbbing wound grew silent and the flickering candles became a motionless moon.

viii

As Rolind retreated from the crypt, Tyre met him at the throne. Morning light colored the marble floor and Rolind peered into the gleaming pearl beads. Then he looked up into the silent man's face.

"Deep below I find great peace, Tyre. It lies beside my brother's corpse. He seems so content, not needing any more comfort than his marble bed. I sense nobility before his presence."

"Do you dream the impossible?"

"The wrong one lies below." For a moment he peered at the crypt door. Then suddenly Jani's accusations resounded in his ears and Rolind broke the silence with a shout.

"Why do you spy on me?"

"Spy, sire?"

"Have I no freedom!" Rolind screamed. "Or is there reason now for constant watch? All around me I fear the minds of a thousand clocks."

"I do not spy. I merely carry your shirt and royal garb." The old man presented the items to the young king. "Today the mourners come to view the corpse of Riis."

"No! It will destroy my peace!"

"It will bring diversion to your mind," the old man lectured. "Already the *Li Scholars* fill the Gazebah with songs of mourning and walk the streets. Here, place these articles upon your back." He helped Rolind don the cape and royal locket.

"They will know that it was I who murdered Dels." Rolind stepped back away from the long bony fingers and looked down into the open vault.

"They have no concern with that. Merely do they carry pity in their hearts and hope of peace. No cruel mind can injure you, for none shall see your sorrow. Here, sit upon your throne. It is yours and all shall know it so."

Rolind sat carefully. Yet, as his discomfort grew, the four councillors entered from his right and, crossing to their seats, nodded to the royal youth, but Rolind looked away. Then Caji swung open the great chamber doors and passed to face his king.

"They climb the hill, sire, and enter soon. There is great solemnity in their walk and compassion in their hearts."

Rolind smiled with great difficulty as Caji stood beside him and Tyre retreated to the gallery.

A procession slowly commenced with each person saying *"Cashi Li"* to the youthful king. And then, with opened Books of Orange, they descended deep into the crypt. So many passing forms lulled the youth into a tranquil mood.

Suddenly within the hall a great clamor arose, forcing Rolind to stare into the faces of a most peculiar group, awkward in their manner and all physically deformed.

A lanky man and one grossly obese woman led the way, with twisted smiles, scars and missing limbs marking others who followed behind them. Then came fifteen midgets and crippled frames. Others pulled a sassal rope and in a creaking wagon sat the blind soothsayer whom Rolind knew, and between his stumps rested a golden harp.

The youth stood up, surprised, and stared at the procession, focusing upon the mournful expression of these freaks. They drew the wooden tram up to the throne. Cautiously, Rolind approached the strange vehicle, smiling at the blind one, excited now to greet the man.

"Have you news for me?" he whispered for only the old one to hear. "Though I laughed before, your words were true."

The deformed mouth issued a creaky voice, the sound much like a whisper.

"As much danger as there exists for me to speak must you be prepared to meet. There are those who are more deformed in thought than I in form."

"Why do you speak to me with such fright?"

"To have said these words may end my life."

Rolind stared deeply at the dull blind eyes.

"And this harp?" He surveyed the broken instrument resting in the legless lap. "Why have you carried it here?"

"It is your *Li,* Rolind, upon which you may also dream. These strings will never break. Come with us and play your song."

"My *Li* is to sit upon that throne." He pointed to the regal chair before them, nervously staring over to where the councillors carefully watched his every move.

"It will never bring you peace. Now we must pass." The cart lurched forward. "Come with us if you wish."

"No!" the frightened ruler screamed. "You cannot leave me suffering like this! NO! NO! It isn't fair that you speak these words, then leave me here to cry!"

Mourners along the way parted and let the procession pass. All singing quickly ceased.

The blind man struck a note and sang:

> My manner is subtle, my fear is deep,
> but you may pluck these strings and sing.
> Their softness is soothing, false *Li* is weak.

And he left Rolind to stand among the crowd. The mourners continued to chant, *"Cashi Li,"* and Rolind turned away in fright. Tyre quickly appeared, and stood beside the boy.

"Their minds are warped. Look, here around you lies the mildness of your reign." Tyre pointed to those who meekly turned to mumble from their Books of Orange.

"But he spoke such truth before. . . ."

"Such is the manner of madmen, Rolind. Come," Tyre pleaded, directing the puzzled boy back into the crowded chamber.

"I want to go below!" he cried as Tyre nudged him forward towards the throne.

"Tonight."

"I do not want to face these people anymore!"

"It is your role." He placed Rolind on the throne. "Here, lean back and dream." His gentle hands relaxed the youth. "Listen to their passing sounds. It will soon become a melody of quietness."

Rolind felt the warm hand leave his shoulder as he reclined, slumped back into his throne, listening to the gentle song of those who passed, and smiling painfully, greeted them back.

IX

A CASTLE GUARD APPROACHED the throne and stood before the king.

"Sire?"

"Yes, Nsi. What words have you? Speak softly in my ear."

The guard approached. "It is Lermo, sire. He awaits an audience."

The boy's face lit up with joy and he excitedly whispered back, "Lead him into my room at once. See that no others follow. I shall come quickly."

X

As Rolind stood within the portal of his room, he viewed the sea captain with a mindful eye: black wide pants with two pairs of finger-width white lines running towards his boots. A bright, clear silk shirt boasted this man's powerful physique and upon his head a broad orange and white plume rose from a three-cornered felt hat. As Rolind looked up at the man's stern and powerful square face, Lermo bowed before the youth.

"Sire . . ."

"I see you admire the saber with which Sinol gifted me."

"Truly Sinol was a master sailor and you were most fortunate in having known the man. His death most surely meant a great loss to all."

Rolind hesitated at the word "death," but the gentle captain's blush made him suddenly at ease.

"Have a seat." Rolind led the man to a writing desk just beyond the obiel. "If there were wine I would offer you a drink. Wait! I'll fetch some."

"Never mind, sire. There is no need for wine."

Rolind slowly returned to the desk and explored the captain's face, seeing within his eyes, an honorable gaze. Lermo looked up to speak.

"Did you not fear to call me to your throne, sire? Most men call me pirate and see dreadfulness in these scars." Rolind followed the contours of a ragged line running from the soft skin beneath the sea captain's eye to the taut skin of his angular chin.

"No." He looked up from the gash. "I see only deep calm within your eyes. Surely it is your confidence which others fear."

Lermo seemed to blush before the boy. "And you, sire, how do you fare?"

Rolind looked toward the flickering candle along the opposite wall, then to the exposed pages of the sacred Book of Orange. He suppressed a tear. As his vision returned to the captain, a wry smile drew across his face.

"I thank you for the flower, Lermo. Truly it is a most cherished gift."

Lermo remained silent.

"It casts life where death now rules aind dissipates the greatest sorrow." Tears swelled beneath the prince's eyes as a momentary thought of Dels flashed through his mind. But he fought back the emotion and stared at the jagged scar across Lermo's chin. His head cocked to follow its path and his voice came with a sullen hush.

"Your scar, Lermo, is it more than just a wound?"

"At one time it burdened me."

"How so?"

Lermo thought back for a moment, then answered: "Before its infliction I was a man unconscious of his limits; then in one quick moment was I devoid of a cherished immortality. Perhaps the realization of my weakness created a man where just a foolish boy had been, suddenly unable to fantasize the elements of the universe."

Rolind stared back, amazed by the words which this gruff-looking man had just spoken.

"I . . . I too bear scars." He slowly looked down, placing a hand across his shirt.

"They will heal," Lermo answered with a calm voice. "So will those which lie beneath the skin."

Rolind turned away, catching sight of the spot where the flower had sat upon the shelf. Then an image of Dels appeared bearing the dancing flower upon his chest.

"There is this man," Rolind spoke up and faced the captain, "who rides the torrid waves. He lives upon a wooden raft. Tell me how he seemed to you."

Lermo was momentarily stopped by the sudden shift, but quickly spoke.

"The old man is either a loon or made of magic. He claims the raft to be an island, yet no crops nor stores lay anywhere in sight. Surely schools of fish do not inhabit such great depths nor forage in such turbulence. When we questioned him regarding land beyond the storm, he merely grinned and offered us entry through it. Yet even he was not foolish enough to drive his raft through the thick clouds, but rode aft the storm. We could see the rain and heard claps of thunder beyond their billows."

"Would he have led you through the storm to find the island beyond?"

"There is no island, sire. Were there, surely nothing grows on it. The rain would wash the soil away and drown every living thing."

"Then from where did the flower come?" demanded Rolind, upset by the captain's casual manner.

"I have no explanation, sire," came the still calm voice.

"Then where one flower grows, surely others flourish."

"I cannot say, sire. Such matters are beyond my knowledge."

"I want to find this place, Lermo! Beyond the storm lies the peace of mind I demand!"

"Sire? Such a place could offer no man peace."

Rolind looked away, dismayed by the captain's words, anxious to have him agree.

"But I had knowledge of the flower before you sent it here. And knowledge of that island which would certainly bring peace to me."

"No, sire. Such vision must be a trick. No eyes could see beyond the storm, no mind could penetrate the blackness with such clarity. The only peace which lies beyond the storm is death."

The captain's declaration disturbed the boy, and Rolind stared deeply into the stern wide eyes.

"There are scars which I must heal. Certainly a remedy will never come when in every vision lies the irritation of my infection! Within these castle walls grows a constant reminder of my own foul deed. The search for peace beyond the storm seems much the better way."

Lermo stared back, his voice sure and calm. "Will not the shadow of its presence appear whenever you seek to hide? Why not merely sail into the free-blown winds? It is peaceful there and the skies are blue."

"Such would only be a temporary peace!"

"And would you wish my men to die when no treasure lies beyond the storm. There is not such desperation in *my* life to fight such a challenge. As I would hesitate to walk into a forest red with fire, so would I hesitate to drive a ship into those rough black seas."

"Then, why did you sail there in the first place?"

"It was a gale which caught my sails and cast us there. Surely I had no plan to engage my men in such a fury. You have received your treasure from that spot, what more do you want?"

"What more do I want? It is peace that I seek! Peace! Peace! Peace! Do you see this hand?" he shouted, exposing his palm before the captain's sight. "Within its grip lies the burdening weight of death! And within my ears, his screams recur and haunt me every moment that I breathe! It is peace I seek! Peace! Nothing more than peace!"

Rolind's voice filled the room as Lermo moved to catch the screaming youth and quell his violent fit with a gentle grip. And he quelled the muffled surge of tears against his chest. Then when Rolind's anguish ceased, Lermo raised his opened hand and brushed the tears away.

"Oh, sire, there is no easy peace, nor lies an easy life aboard our ship."

Rolind looked up, made more anxious by the captain's words.

"Many times the harshness of the crew would make you wish yourself away and often find no gentle things to say. And were they ever to know your name, perhaps your safety would be held too sacred and would interfere with our manner on the waves."

Then Rolind's tears ceased, and he felt a strength grow within and faced the man who stood before him.

"Surely the name of Leci can offer these men no reason to suspect. My garb of common clothes can hide my royal frame, and an apprenticeship be regarded as my role aboard the ship. Truly it will be a most profitable experience to learn of the sea and search the treasure of the storm."

"And when words are passed which may offend thy royal ears?"

"I shall laugh or turn away."

"It could be dangerous, sire."

Rolind turned to face the sky beyond the obiel. A distant bird circled high above and the young king peered deeply into the curtain of sky-blue light.

"Many times my games and dreams have been those of ships. It is in my blood, you know. We Merus have always been great men of the sea!"

Lermo hesitated. Then after a moment of thought he nodded with a distant look of approval. Rolind quickly drew the captain to his desk and spoke of plans and agreed to meet before tomorrow's morn grew old.

XI

As LERMO LEFT, Rolind approached the obiel, and glancing across the blue-green waters of the sea, he breathed triumphantly at his chance to succeed with the plan to find the flower and happiness. For the first time in so long a while, the boy smiled contentedly and felt much at ease.

As he stood before the windows, Vernon entered from the rear.

"Sire, I bring you food your mother prepared."

Rolind slowly turned to face the white-haired councillor.

"Why does she herself not carry these here?"

Vernon ignored the boy's question. He laid the tray upon the writing table beside the obiel and beckoned the young king to sit. Rolind followed the old man's movements as the odor of fowl and beets enticed his appetite. He approached the steaming food, picking off large bits of fleshy meat. Then sitting down to eat, he quickly forgot his original words.

His hunger was quelled, and then Vernon spoke without looking around.

"The birds fly high."

Rolind looked up. "Do you refer to their games or make suspicious prophecy about my pending trip?"

"Sire?" Vernon turned and faced the king. "Why, these are merely words. They have no meaning beyond themselves."

"And were yesterday's thoughts in the Council Room mere words, too?"

Vernon's head sank as the idea reached his ears.

"Perhaps, young sire, there exists no such thing as mere words. Perhaps they truly reflect our deepest thoughts and personal perceptions, leaving us unmasked before the shrewdest mind." Then turning back to survey the confines of the kingdom, he added, "Along the tableland live Taiu, Vriu, Nesu, Casu, Alsu, Kinu and others whose fields and villages flourish with their art and style. While beyond the ragged mountans to the north awaits our enemy." Again he turned to face the young king. "It is the Bintu who seek our death and intimidate our lives. Even our neighboring kingdoms beyond the sea and along the northern mountains fear their presence."

"And why do you speak thusly at this time? Is it to remind me of our history and to argue against my plans?"

"I speak thusly to remind you that three hundred years of Byui kings have solidified our tribes into a fortress against the Bintu. Within our boundaries is a home where we may raise our children in our own way. And not since Bintu warriors stood frustrated at the palisade cliffs hundreds of years ago have our tribes more reason to live in fear. Once they drove us hard, Meru and Gimbu tribes alike, driving us out of those peaceful and fertile plains beyond the mountains, then across the flat tableland with a Bintu plan to drown us in the sea."

Rolind looked over towards the glowing candle above the Book of Orange, then over towards the palisade, visualizing the Meru and Gimbu tribes shimmying down sassal ropes, carrying children and aiding their women, guiding their store-goods over the newly discovered cliff refuge before their Bintu tormentors could launch another attack against the makeshift camps which overlooked the sea.

"Had it not been for that frustration at the cliffs, Meru might never have existed today," Vernon continued.

"Why do you remind me of all this!" Rolind demanded.

"It is a lesson for your life. Had these early men not withstood the pressure of constant siege and had they not used the limited resources of the Gazebah and the few oases in this torrid strip of coarse rocky shelf, their surrender would have meant certain death to them and their king; and the infant colony which bred this kingdom would have died. Had they not continued to struggle against their tormentors and hardships, never could they have driven back the Bintu nor could those other tribes who sought a refuge from these hoards of barbaric cutthroats been able to survive. Each helped the other and fought together, though perhaps one tribe did suffer more than another."

"But after the Bintu left, these tribes made battle amongst themselves for a hundred years, killing off each other's kings and councils."

"It was their nature as men to fight! But once a leader was proclaimed, the bloodshed ceased and children learned respect for other tribes. The House of Byui was ordained with that power of protection."

Rolind looked away.

"And it is still entrusted now to you, Rolind! That is why you are the king! And as our history is filled with pain, so is yours, and as our people found its resolution, so shall you."

Rolind stared into the pleading man's eyes, then glanced at the saber of Sinol above his bed, then across to the Book of Orange.

"Just as the horror of our history is enshrined in that Book," Rolind proclaimed, pointing to the open pages, "so the horror of my deed is imprinted in my mind."

"You must learn to turn back the tide of onslaught and rebuild the fortress which makes you a man," Vernon pleaded. "The lesson of history written within is not one of defeat, but the story of men who rose again."

"But I am not that strong!" Rolind protested. "I cannot rebuild from what was destroyed!"

"But you can. You are so different from any other man. Had the ancient tribes chosen defeat, we would not be here today."

"Perhaps it would have been better that way!"

Vernon stood transfixed, and amidst the silence, Rolind's own words echoed in his mind. The youth grew calm and shook his head in disagreement with his very words. Then Vernon approached and offered up softly-spoken words.

"The tribal elders sojourn to council here and to bid their new king strength. By such a manner they seek their own strength and thus the power of our defense. Amongst them shall come the comfort which you yourself search out. Beneath the Bintu threat shall we mutually find the strength to overcome our pain."

"But their quest for peace makes no common bond with me!"

"Only in the circumstance from which it springs, does the search for peace begin. But, never think this need unique."

Vernon's words stilled the boy's argumentative mind and made him think, and with opened palm upon Rolind's shoulder he offered him still a deeper peace.

"Perhaps I am merely a councillor to the king, but in my heart do I see my own son before these eyes. Heed my words, Rolind dear, never hide away in terror. To draw a veil across your mind would be to lose whatever joy the universe might bring. Seek your peace here, nearby, and consider those who suffer by your side."

Rolind swung around, knocking Vernon's hand away. "I do not need another father! One was enough! From now on *I* shall choose my friends."

"Why do you act so hard on the outside when inside you cry so loud. Is there no trust left within you?"

"And tell me," Rolind wheeled around, "whom should I trust? He who murdered my peace, or they who permitted him to act?"

"There is none other to blame than that *one*. And realize that your father now lies deep within his own death."

"When Plio spoke of treachery, did he speak in jest?"

"If such questions rile you, sire, then remain and search them out."

"And who would you suspect, Vernon? Or do you simply make prognosis on whims? Do you believe in Plio's words? Answer me!"

"It is hard to say, sire. Many of his words make sense, much of his conjecture leaves doubts."

"Why won't you answer me straight, Vernon?" the boy demanded.

"How can I, sire? They are logical thoughts, yet it is too early for rashness. Whom do we accuse? How can we know? If only you would remain here can we hope to find a remedy."

"First you accuse Tyre, then you beg me to stay because you fear the Bintu."

"Such proposals are not unfair."

"Then you doubt even your own thoughts and those of Plio."

"I have never made accusations, sire, but only caution you of what dangers lie around us all."

"No! I will not remain. You yourself can answer the queries of the elders. They can remain here until my return. You will think of something. You're very good at plotting thoughts in other people's minds."

"Sire!"

Suddenly a figure caught the eye of Vernon and he turned to face the intruder. As Tyre entered, Vernon shouted out, "How dare you intrude in here! The councillor's flag hangs upon the door. You know the limits of your freedom!"

Tyre stopped to face his accuser. Rolind also looked up, staring at the councillor by his side, aghast at the sudden shout.

"Tell me, Tyre," Vernon continued, "why do you remain when no prince exists to teach? Is it your plan to interfere with the young king's role?"

"I remain by request of the king. There is no intention but my concern for his peace of mind. I have no cause to interfere."

"But you just did!" He pointed at the orange- and red-striped flag draped upon the door.

"I must assure you that indeed it was an accident caused solely by my failing vision. My eyes grow weaker with each passing year. There is no cause for alarm, I shall leave."

Tyre turned away from Vernon's eyes to humbly face the king. "I feel that I have troubled you, sire. Forgive me please. There is no malice in my will."

"Tell us why you came," Rolind said.

"To mention that the Gimbu elders sit within the public chamber, sire."

Rolind looked around at Vernon, pleased with the mentor's explanation, awaiting the councillor's accusation to give him cause for rebuttal in front of the guardian-teacher. But the three remained transfixed until Tyre finally stepped back and commenced to leave.

"I have no more to say," Tyre stated to Vernon, then quickly left the room.

As the door closed, Vernon met the fury of the youthful king.

"You have no right to speak to Tyre in such a manner! He is my friend, almost dear enough to be my father!"

"That is no reason for such trust," Vernon warned the angry youth. "Just as you claimed fear of your father's mind, so you must make your distrust universal until the culprit of your thoughts is found."

"You confuse me."

"And if there was not a suddenness of fear within my mind when Tyre did intrude, I might have invited him to wine and discuss the matter confidentially with him."

"How dare you speak such vindication! Neither were you invited at this time, Vernon! The mourning of my father's death march below. Surely you should be down there to entertain the elders and scholars of the *Li* who wish to express their sadness."

"As much as is your role," Vernon shrewdly countered.

Rolind stared at the man, realizing his inability to argue successfully.

"I concede. Here I agree with you. Give me a moment alone, then I shall greet the mourners before my throne."

Vernon nodded approval of Rolind's plan and left the room.

Rolind watched the door close behind the councillor, then returning to the windows of the obiel, viewed the rocking ships below. An image of Lermo's rough face appeared before his eye and a smile, filled with his own self-assurance of decision, played across his face.

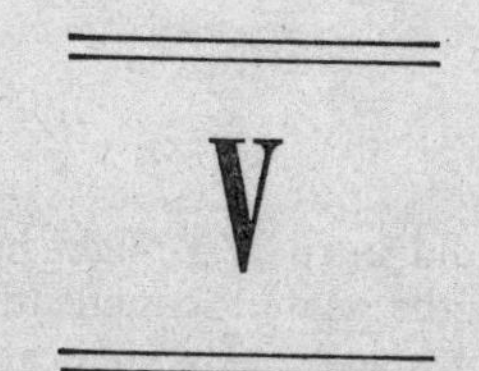

i

THAT MORNING before the sun had risen and all still slept, save the royal guards who blocked the portcullis before the castle, Rolind laid the royal locket and his golden crown upon the Book of Orange. Only for a moment did he survey the words which had haunted him those many years. Then he turned and fled, scurrying down the corridors and into his black, secret maze. When he reached the turn where lately had the candle danced and brought him back to kill, nothing blocked his way.

As he emerged from the crypt, soft morning hues cast his form into a shadow along the pinnacle, a flowing rhythm around the path of rocks and shrubs. And though still burdened in his mind, he donned his disguise of blue and white cloth. Then amidst the brightness of a gold-flame dawn, the anxious youth hurried along the cobblestone road to the seaport. Whereupon he saw the captain, Lermo, and an oarscrew of three. And though he wished to surrender to their care, he acted ignorant of the man and quickly walked on by.

"Capture that youth," the captain's voice rang out. "Offer him wage and board and tell him apprenticeship aboard the *Voyager* serves better for his life than to sleep here in the streets."

A large man, most gentle in manner and sporting a grizzly beard stopped the youth's advance. Rolind made no move to escape and listened to the proposal. Then he looked around, exploring the scene as though contemplating the seaman's words.

"I see no danger in it," he concluded. "Perhaps one day I can wear the black-striped silks of your captain and one day be your master, too, and offer some other youth a way to free himself from the daily hunger of the streets."

"You are a clown, young man," the seaman said and laughed. "Perhaps our work will make a man of you, a man with arms much stronger than those of the frail young lady I might seek along the banks at night. To become a captain may be another thing. But come along. Who really knows your future? Do you have a trade?"

"Just my youth."

"Fine, you will learn one aboard our ship."

The bay waters rested still and the small oarsboat ran smoothly. As it reached the three-masted merchant ship, a rope ladder landed near the boy-king and one of the oarsmen coaxed him to scale aboard the tall wooden vessel. At first Rolind felt uneasy beneath its sway, but as he reached the top and climbed over the railing rope, he became lost in the activity of men hurrying aboard, some climbing the masts to position themselves along the yards, others untying weather-beaten ropes which held still the long furled sails. As the flying sails were dropped and tied, loud slaps echoed in the wind and the ship lurched forward. Rolind fought to remain upright.

"Come along," Lermo called to the youth, leading him along the slippery surface to a small round-roofed structure located on the rearmost deck. Light creaked through the small square windows of this dark wood cabin, and as Lermo sat behind an oak table, a large cutlass on the starboard wall made Rolind turn in fear. As he nervously began to sit upon a small stool at the center of the room Lermo shouted out, "You will remain standing!"

Rolind backed up, afraid.

"There will be no informality in my presence. Mansano," he said pointing behind the boy to a tall, powerful Kinu whose right hand rested on the handle of a bull whip, "will be your chief. You will take orders from him. Make no mistakes and learn quickly. Death awaits slackers and the sea has no friends."

"Come along," the gruff voice called and though Rolind hesitated, desperately wishing to speak to Lermo to determine whether the man feigned or actually offered up a threat, he found the captain gone. Reluctantly he followed Mansano out to the deck.

The salty wind slapped Rolind's cheeks, and large high

clouds floated beyond the mast tops. Seagulls circled around the bow. The uneasy rocking made the youth feel a bit sick, and though he wished to turn around and find a more stable place, Mansano led him straight to a group of five who sat among wide rolls of sassal. Then handing Rolind a frayed end of rope, he ordered the youth: "Watch this man braid the ends. And weave tightly! That line may hold your life tonight." He turned and left the boy standing before the working group.

For a moment Rolind watched the others work, then without words kneeled down beside the nearest sailor and began to free the three small bundles contained in the main line.

"Uh." He looked around, afraid of making an error. "How far down is sufficient?"

A hollow eye socket looked up at him. "This far, muffet," came its sandy voice as the scraggly bearded old man revealed an eight-inch segment of line. "Does your mother know you're here?"

"Huh?" Rolind backed away, trying not to stare at the deformed flap of skin. "Thanks." He turned away, trying to ignore the man, and began another end.

"No talk?" persisted the creature. "You frightened or something? Maybe this eye." He pointed at the scarred hollow. "Could be like you tomorrow. No way to know." Then looking away from Rolind he spoke solemnly. "Seamen ugly, but friendly . . ."

The seaman's expression of defeat made Rolind feel at ease and as he looked back to view the stranger, he spoke in apologetic tones.

"I hear that the ocean teems with fish to fill my belly." The hidden face quickly revealed itself again.

"So . . . you read."

The statement surprised Rolind and he stared back at the man.

"Better start weaving, boy. Mansano whips hard," and he handed Rolind a length of rope.

Rolind's cautious smile received a warm one in return. The stocky Gimbu began to lay strand over strand and Rolind imitated his every move. Eventually strands became an end of rope and Rolind smiled with pride. The friendly voice tried to encourage him on, but Rolind turned away. As his attention drew across the deck and beyond the bow, searching familiar sights along the shore, a figure suddenly blocked his view: a sinister pair of eyes.

The stranger squatted between Rolind and the one-eyed man, revealing a curved-tip knife. Quietly he chipped up pieces of the hardwood deck. Rolind explored the slender but powerful bulge of muscles and the scenes of naked women and bloody daggers tatooed along each vein. Then he explored the scar beneath his chin.

"Who's this one, Kaiso? A new pet to frighten?"

"Muffet, I call it," the older man smiled. "It eats fish."

The newcomer bellowed out loud, and then abruptly stopped and frightened Rolind with a hideous gaze.

"And does it think?"

"It reads, and now braids rope."

"Beware, Muffet." The newcomer stared grimly at Rolind. "Kaiso has scars behind that hollow socket, and he has no *Li*."

Rolind looked away, uncomfortable with this stranger's presence, avoiding his two peering eyes. And as the grim stranger arose Rolind held his breath, afraid of what might come, but the other simply moved away. When only Kaiso sat by his side, Rolind picked up a length of rope and continued with his task. He remained cautious, surveying the deck, watching the others who passed, expecting others to disturb his peace.

But none around seemed to pay him heed and once again Rolind began to feel comfortable staring out in the direction of the quickly fading palisades. The sky behind the wall of rock appeared a pastel yellow surrounded by a light blue halo as the sun continued rising in its arc. And no longer did the cawking of seagulls ring above the ship.

"Seek your mother, Muffet?" Kaiso called. "She gone now."

Rolind strained to see the castle but it lay beyond his sight. And he smiled contendedly, then sat back, turning to watch Kaiso demonstrate a weak weave which he had made. Rolind strained to join the ends.

The sun blazed strong, but the sea spray cooled and the clipping waves played rhythmically against the hull's wooden planks. The winds plucked bass sounds through the shrouds. And when he had completed a splice, Kaiso approved.

"Children drown in water. Good splice, Muffet. Now, another . . ."

Rolind began to smile at last.

The touch of coarse, wet rope was becoming comfortable within his grip, and though his arms ached from fatigue, the splices became much tighter. When the sun stood at its zenith, a sailor dressed in white and blue and carrying a leather pouch approached the deck where Rolind and Kaiso worked. He handed all but Rolind thin strips of dried white fish and handfuls of dried fruit. As Rolind watched, Kaiso accepted a portion. The youth could feel the hollow of his stomach and looked hungrily around. His mouth filled with saliva. Then the food-bearer spoke to Kaiso:

"Does your pet eat salty fish?"

"Maybe it'll grow when fed." Kaiso looked back at Rolind with a smile, "Looks sick now. Better feed it quick."

Rolind smiled deeply at his one-eyed friend, then gladly accepted two strips of fish. Gnats circled his fist. Then small bits of dried apricots and pineapple bounced into his open palms. He broke off a piece of fish with his teeth and sucked it hard, extracting the taste and feeling satisfied of hunger, and as he looked up, the land behind them was gone and only sea swayed around the gliding ship.

Rolind sat in a semicircle surrounded by seven other men. He listened to them chew, and explored the gruesome scars across their faces. A one-armed man sat whistling.

A few spoke, but not many words passed. And Tiki, the pixie troubadour who had brought the magic flower to the boy, sat above the crew upon the quarterdeck hatch and sang a happy ditty. Some of the men joined in and Kaiso coaxed the boy to sing:

There once was a monkey as proud as a lad
who carried his tail in a bow,

There once was a monkey as proud as a lad
  who carried his tail in a bow.

Once on a ship he did steal, a brave castaway
  who carried his tail in a bow,
Once on a ship he did steal, a brave castaway
  who carried his tail in a bow.

When the crew they did find him,
    a great cheer they gave
  though he carried his tail in a bow,
When the crew they did find him,
    a great cheer they gave
  though he carried his tail in a bow.

One night the stars gathered and made quite a show
  though he carried his tail in a bow,
One night the stars gathered and made quite a show
  though he carried his tail in a bow,

As the maiden of moonlight did call out his name
  he carried his tail in a bow
As the maiden of moonlight did call out his name
  he carried his tail in a bow.

Had he not been concerned with the bow in his tail
  perhaps he could sleep with her now,
Had he not been concerned with the bow in his tail
  perhaps he could sleep with her now.

More fish and fruit filled Rolind's belly that night, and above the constant sound of crashing wave against wood, Tiki plucked his mandolin. Lermo stood outside his cabin for a while, staring through a sextant. Then he quickly retreated behind the closed door. Rolind listened to the winds slap the wide mainsails; an almost full moon and millions of stars filled the blackness overhead, and the thick, sweet wine warmed his ears.

"Lots to learn, Muffet. Now you sleep deep."

Kaiso led the boy to the forecastle, a large single-story house with a rounded roof. Within, the musty odor of sweat and salt water struck his senses. The strong moon cast light enough for him to see the tiers of hammocks, some already filled with snoring men. Kaiso unravelled a hammock towards the front.

"You sleep here. Two sleep below you. The sun wakes you in the morning."

Rolind hoisted himself into the sassal framework. The tough strands held his shoulder blades positioned and contoured around his frame. And though he tried to lay awake, afraid of dreaming, the stillness of night and the rhythmic rocking sea drew the tired body into deep sleep.

The sun and the sounds of arousing men woke Rolind the next morning and he looked beyond his rope cradle at the overcrowded chamber. A short, large-headed man approached the still groggy youth, and others closer to the entranceway faced them.

"Do you make battle in your sleep, or should we call to port and fetch you a maiden?"

Great laughter filled his ears as Rolind realized the starkness of his dreams and felt the dried teardrops upon his cheeks. He turned away from the laughing crowd.

"Th . . . they are dreams, nothing more," he apologized to the one before him.

"Come, Muffet." Kaiso's voice called beyond the crowd. "There is work to do for the next few days. Much rope to braid, much sail to sew."

ii

For two more nights his mind was filled with rage; he would be wakened by his brother's deathly scream and would stare wide-eyed across the void of night to watch that endless dagger fight and see his brother die again. And when the blood would flow, would he sit limp-shouldered in his sling, mindlessly swayed by the rocking sea. Then would he moan, then weep, then fall into dreamless sleep.

And beneath the sun each day Rolind sewed sails, braided sassal strands into rope and stood before the leeward railing in vigilant search across limitless waves, searching for some break in the calm, searching for turbulent waters and black, thundering clouds. But naught did he see. And when his eyes would drop in disappointment, Kaiso's hand would lead him back to the ceaseless routine of work. Whatever Rolind did, he would find this smiling, frog-voiced Kaiso by his side, encouraging him to find some pleasure in his day. But when his stitches grew long and the space between each braid seemed like endless stretches of time Rolind could sense a constant surveillance of eyes across the deck. And though he would frantically turn to locate each face, only could he find the blank, hollow forms of men walking by. Kaiso would sit beside the youth, speaking words of comfort; his broken voice becoming a song, a soothing rhythm to the boy.

Whenever the hours grew long, Rolind would search the deck for Lermo's scar and his colorful plume, hoping at first that the man would approach him and offer some explanation as to why the trip was taking so long. But not once did the man appear! And whenever Rolind tried to see beyond the constantly closed door of the captain's cabin he would find the awesome eyes of Mansano peering back. Soon the boy-king imagined Captain Lermo in plot against his sanity. Then how his hatred grew! Yet whenever he turned swelled-chest to face the whip-carrying Kinu, and felt to cry, Kaiso offered his mind diversion with a rope to braid. But when the one-eyed sailor ceased to speak, Rolind dreamed on, envisioning himself tearing the whip from Mansano's grip and standing within the captain's space, demanding Lermo to reveal his plan. But in his dream the man refused to speak and Rolind found himself unleashing his anger and tearing the flesh away from Lermo's face. Kaiso's touch would fade away the scene and leave the boy in shaking fear.

On the third day, as the crew gathered for its meal, voices grumbled and daggers chipped the deck. Rolind turned his own anger towards the stoic Kinu who stood before the captain's door. A sudden voice awoke his mind.

"This course is nonsense! We sail too far from land for safety in this merchant ship. And look," the sailor said, facing the bow, pointing to the single triangular sail of the bowspirit. "He flies the lateen for extra speed. This captain of ours drinks too much rum for clear thought."

"Would he risk his own life, fool?" another said while breaking off a piece of jerky with rotted teeth.

"A fool am I? Thirty years at sea makes me no fool, merely wise and cautious."

"He is right, Nidok," another called out. "We head north by north-west and already too far from land. The Linus sail these routes and their pirates infest the waves. Methinks the captain sails for personal glut. To be cast away by storm makes no man complain, but to openly expose ourselves is mad! I for one will keep my dagger sharp and watch the stars. I fear we head back to those thick gray clouds and that lunatic sage. Perhaps our captain seeks more flowers to appease our king."

Rolind looked away, abashed by the thought.

"Methinks it stinks!" another voice spoke up.

"Bah!" another complained and arose to spit into the wind.

A loud snap echoed off the deck. All eyes turned. Mansano stood before the group, staring coldly at each man. Rolind avoided the Kinu's deep-set eyes.

"Does the food cause aches or is it mutiny you plan?"

"No, Mansano," one man cooly answered. "We only pass the time in chatter."

"Get back to your chores and chatter in your sleep! Speak of women, not of Lermo's mind."

Rolind turned with fear and begged some comfort from Kaiso. But before he could speak, the old man stood up.

"Come, Muffet, rope needs weaving. Much to do if storms come."

The hours passed and once again Rolind's mind grew restless. He approached the sea, staring out to find some sign of that distant storm, standing there thoughtless before the railing of the center deck. The salt spray slapped his skin. And as he stared into the rolling waves a vision of Dels appeared. He closed his eyes and turned away. An eerie voice stopped him.

"Who are you, young one?"

Rolind faced a tall, wide-faced sailor, and wished to be away from the row of broken teeth.

"Kaiso calls you Muffet, but your cries at night are unnatural. They spook us more than the edge of our sea. It makes us suspicious, young one."

"Of . . . of what?" the youth stepped back, afraid of being addressed as sire.

"Perhaps you are a demon sent here from beneath the sea."

"Of what do you speak?" He looked away, confused by the idea and afraid of the stare.

A second man grabbed his friend's arm and spun him around. "Hush, man! Such talk will certainly rile Lermo. He will cast you to your death."

"But," the other protested, "this small creature is no marine, yet he sails with us. And suddenly our course is strange." Then he turned his attention back towards Rolind. "Does Lermo plot a private course for you? Is yours a special *Li* which serves our master?"

"I—I have no knowledge of your thoughts," Rolind quickly interceded, afraid of being known.

"You are wrong, Nuso," the second man said to his friend. "The young one before us has no *Li*. That is why Kaiso watches over him, and why he cries at night." And turning back towards Rolind, he said, "There does lay terror in your heart and you seek absolution from your fears."

"No, Xerrtio! Do not speak any more!"

Nuso pushed his comrade aside. "We can trust this one. He needs our aid."

Rolind wished to be away, but Nuso stepped in front of him, blocking the boy's retreat and staring into his eyes. The stranger offered up a suddenly comforting smile.

"Of course he can be trusted. Look how his eyes avoid mine and how nervously he twitches. A spy would stand comfortably. Tonight, young lad, when it is dark and the hammocks filled, I shall awaken you, and reveal the way to peace. Speak nothing of this to any other, especially that Tiki. He is a spy and in those songs he sings are codes which only Lermo understands. Now, be away, for long speech will certainly raise suspicion."

ROLIND SPENT THAT DAY AND NIGHT in constant turmoil; not wishing to trust the two who had approached him on the deck, but finding too much truth within their declarations. Indeed he suffered greatly and he sought some comfort for his mind. And also the fear that Lermo plotted against his life made him see the captain much as he had once seen his father. And as he tossed within his hammock, wishing Tyre there to help him out, a figure rudely approached and silently beckoned the hysteric youth to follow him. And without a thought or protest Rolind traversed the moon-bathed deck and then found himself led down through the forward hatch, deep into the hull where barrels and larger boxes of cargo filled the space. In a clearing almost to the bowline twenty men sat in a wide circle: three long boxes were laid as a table in the center. Rolind recognized only a few, for most had been the quiet men aboard, passing unnoticed on the deck. One man shot to his feet and Rolind froze as he recognized the face: the one who had chipped the deck planks with his blade.

"Why have you brought *him* here?" the protest came.

"For he is without a *Li* and seeks peace within his life."

"He cannot be trusted! He is Kaiso's pet!"

"He is here, Biano. Just as you were once a foundling to our cause."

"But he is strange," Biano begged. From beside the makeshift table he stared deeply into Rolind's eyes. "Look around you, boy, and see twenty corpses should you speak to any of this night."

Rolind caught the stares of all within the space: oil lamps above his head cast deep shadows across each face.

"I could never cause death again," he pleaded, suddenly aware of the words just spoken, and suddenly afraid they would make him speak.

"Aha! So you have murdered before," Biano called out and laughed. "Then truly do you belong among us here," and calmly returned to his seat.

"I refuse to speak of it!" Rolind shouted, turning away.

"Truly we are all brothers then," Nuso spoke as he warmly touched Rolind's shoulder. The others began a solemn chant.

Kana li ti nijo
Asa mini canna
Nasana illi asa
Kana li ti nijo

The words made no sense to Rolind, but he listened carefully, peering through the dull yellow light. The men completed the chant three times. Then as quiet came, Nuso spoke to him.

"Kana is the power of the universe. We fear it and seek appeasement of its awesome might. It is Kana which causes all our pain in life, and our rituals and chants ward off the death which Kana holds before each man. And to die without enjoyment of continual pain is to perish unto Kana after life. It is only after a most torturous death can a man be strong enough to tolerate the Kana's eternal hate."

Rolind stared at those before him, realizing no escape, and meekly sat upon an empty barrel. Nuso withdrew a dagger from its sheath and, after laying it upon the floor, raised one pant leg to the knee. Rolind stared at the skin. Scars ran the length of Nuso's calf and as the man lifted the dagger, he drew its tip along the flesh, slowly cutting diagonally across the other scabs. Blood oozed and Rolind turned away. But as Dels' face flashed before him he turned back to face the crew. And before him every other in the hull performed upon himself the act which Nuso had done. Rolind, sickened by the sight, fell to his side, vomiting, wishing to escape.

But Nuso raised him up and said, "We here are not cruel men. But Kana is more to be feared than even our own pain. Those who do not demonstrate their strength will fall victim to Kana's power after life. For you to overcome the fear within your mind, you must first overcome the pain. Then shall you have no more conflicts in life. The strength against Kana will fill your mind."

Rolind stared back at Nuso. The man wore a pleasing smile.

"Your pain, where is it?" Rolind begged.

"Kana has received it with his greed, and he has been appeased. And these men here—look at those before you. They too smile, though surely our act may seem vile and you turned away."

The others did indeed bare sincerest smiles across their faces. Then a flask of rum went to each man and they cleansed their wounds.

Once again the chant began:

Kana li ti nijo
Asa mini canna
Nasana illi asa
Kana li ti nijo

and though their voices commenced in a muffled tone, the beat increased to a manic pace.

Kana li ti nijo
Asa mini canna
Nasana illi asa
Kana li ti nijo

Nuso offered Rolind a small round leaf. "Chew this and savor its peculiar taste." He watched each man lift a leaf and place it on the tongue.

"I am just an observer," Rolind pleaded.

"Surely the taste of a simple spice can do no harm."

Rolind accepted the fuzzy leaf, and hesitantly laid it on his tongue. The minty taste enticed him on.

"Another," Nuso coaxed. "It will ease you."

As the chant intensified in his ears, Rolind accepted another leaf, soon feeling light and suddenly afoot without reason. The others in the dimly lit room drank deeply of the rum and each arose, chanting more rapidly, spinning and dancing to some inaudible but frenzied beat.

Rolind suddenly reached for the floor, sharp pains piercing his brain, and as he wheeled around on all fours, found himself staring into the flickering oil lamp, his tongue hanging loosely, his extremities lacking sensation. The lamp flame greatly intense in brilliance; its heat like that of a great furnace before him. And as he stared into its light, time seemed non-existent, and reality, a blur.

A distant noise made Rolind conscious again and he struggled to reach out and touch it with his mind. But it had come as a momentary and fuzzy sound. Then he reached out to touch his mouth but couldn't seem to reach the lips. Then he blindly felt around, searching for some object to hoist himself against and lift himself up. And as he found himself erect, suddenly he could see, peering into a circle of men. Through the cloud which blocked clear vision and a deafness which had blocked all sound, Rolind perceived that Nuso held a knife up high and that the others seemed to thrash long black belts against the air before them.

Then with wobbly legs, Rolind lifted himself atop a wooden box to locate the object of their flagellations, his mind still swirling as he fought for balance and bodily control. The slapping sounds seemed sharp-edged and the light reflected off moving arms appeared like blurs, silhouettes of motion. Rolind peered between two men, his eyes frozen before the spectacle.

There lay a nude man, not held by any other. Large black welts and deep bloody gashes were tatooed across his chest, legs and arms. Leather straps continued to strike the rippling skin, the body writhing beneath each blow. Yet the mouth continued to smile as though in earnest enjoyment of the act. Rolind surveyed the taut, drawn eyes, the wide-stretched cheeks and the pleasure-lapping tongue. Then without a cue Nuso came down hard with the silver blade as the others drew back and instantly ceased their strikes. The blade ripped cleanly through the chest. And Rolind stared up into the victim's wince of death, but it passed in a moment, as though the sailor had longed for that moment, a smile of contentment suddenly overcame his face and limply his head dropped over.

The boy suddenly felt devoid of legs and toppled from

his place, his head landing hard against the wooden floor. His fall seemed unending, his eyes reaching deeper and deeper into darkness, a dull sensation of pain becoming so intense as to numb all sensation and make it feel limitless.

iv

ROLIND AWOKE ALONE in the darkened hull. His head throbbed and a burning itch along his calf forced him to unravel his loose-fitting pant leg. A dagger wound was gouged along the main muscle body. His eyes opened in fright, his head nodded in disbelief around him. He searched for some sign of what he had experienced just that night before, a misplaced box, a drop of blood, his own illness, a piece of clothing, anything!

But he held back the terror and ran, knocking into crates and barrels and finally he climbed the damp rope ladder onto the quarter-deck and into the glaring sun. There he fell against some rope lying on the deck and turned away from those who passed, not daring to cry, sitting openmouthed and afraid to think. But the sight of Mansano produced intense fear and he quickly rose and hurried along the deck, hitting the railing and catching himself before he could fall again. The sounds of heavy footsteps made him peer in every direction, afraid that someone would spot his strange behavior and make him speak. As he cowered along the deck, Tiki's song made him stop.

What does the birdie seek
as this chilly day begins,
a loose cardage or sail,
or a human freak?

Rolind searched the mainsail yard, hoping to spot Nuso or Biano, then suddenly looked back at Tiki, realizing the truth cast in the pixie's words. He turned away, afraid to scream.

Mansano's whip struck near the boy-king and the huge

man barked, "No food for lazy men! There is sail to mend on the aft deck! Get to it!" Rolind quickly fled.

But as he reached the foremast and his eyes cleared, Rolind could make out Biano on the quarterdeck sewing sail. He stopped, afraid to approach the distant man. A whooshing sound passed his ear and then a solid thump resounded by his leg. A dagger stuck into the deck alongside his scarred leg. Rolind froze at the sight. When he dared to stare up and look above, he could find only five men moving along the foremast yard inspecting the ropes which stretched the billowed sail wide. And he ran, afraid suddenly to stop and see Mansano approaching. He peered at the awesome whip, hurrying to where Biano and the others mended sail.

A sailor handed him a small curved herring rib with a strand of flax running through the eye on the flat side of the bone and Rolind faced away from Biano's stare. He quietly followed the others sewing upon the salty-dried sail. His fingers twitched out of control and he nervously looked about.

"Make your stitches smaller," an old sailor snapped. Without looking up, Rolind obeyed.

"Have you sewn your tongue, Muffet?" another said.

"I–I feel a bit ill . . ."

A more gentle voice dispelled Rolind's apprehension for a moment until another spoke. "The tea appears more rough today. . . . You did not use your hammock last night. It was quiet enough for me to dream about my woman last night."

"And disturb us with your chatter this morning," another interrupted. Some of the men nearby laughed.

"Did Mansano make you keep the watch as punishment for your youth?" another interceded as Rolind looked up, confused.

"Beware this one, Muffet," a man along the railing called out, pointing at the last speaker. "Koli will say sweet things and make you feel at ease; then while you sleep, destroy your innocence with open hand. He dreams each man a maiden for his passion."

Others laughed but Koli drew a dagger, his face steaming with anger.

"Cease your games, pigs!" the caustic old man shouted and stepped between the two.

His attention quickly returned to the squatting youth. Rolind tried to look away.

"Tell us, Muffet . . . where did you sleep last night?"

Rolind cast a momentary glance towards Biano but the man stared as though equally curious.

"M—my dreams haunted me. I chose to stare into the darkness beyond the bowsprit rather than cry into your ears. The wind and spray set my mind at ease."

"And the murder? Were you at peace enough to hear it?"

A great roar from the men startled Rolind.

"What murder?" they asked.

The old man continued to speak.

"Last night Topet was cast overboard. His blood lies upon the starboard rail. And you, Muffet, what do you know?"

"Nothing," he pleaded, looking up at the silent crew around him.

"It is these Bintus!" Koli declared.

"Bintus?" Rolind exclaimed. "Do Bintus sail a Meru ship?" He rose to face the others, surprised by the idea, turning to peer disbelieving at Biano; a sudden chill struck his back.

"Ah, if only the king knew; surely he would sink this merchant ship!"

"Bah!" another exclaimed. "They scourge every ship within our fleet."

"It would have been better to have killed them all. Instead, that fool Lermo tied their legs and worked them on the yards. Servants, indeed!"

"But Lermo thought they were Lidus," another swore. "How could he have known they were really Bintu scum, having scuttled a Lidu ship and driven her hulk hard to sink our rig! Even I thought they were Lidu pirates till Xedan told Mansano of his conversion, the dog! He himself whipped a poor human to his death, then cast him overboard!"

"The bastard was a Bintu!" interrupted the old man.

"No matter! Xedan murdered!"

Rolind looked into the faces of those who argued and

saw nothing but anger. The sail lay unattended upon the deck, the herringbone needles scattered along its surface. The wound slightly irritated the boy and he wished to scratch it, but feared the others would suspect his knowledge of the human sacrifice.

"I for one have no tolerance for them, Muffet," a threatening voice said from the railing. "Fifteen of us caught them in the hold during their frenzied dance one night and we slit their throats. They hung from the foremast yard for five days."

Rolind turned sharply and stared back at Biano. The Bintu stood calmly alongside the unworked sail.

"Enough!" the old man barked.

Rolind looked around. Koli approached. The boy stepped away, afraid, but the sailor spoke in gentle tones. "This sea is a terrible place, Muffet. It has an eye in the moon to tantalize your fears, it has a voice in the wind which sings, yet it learns more than a man can speak. And it has claws in every wave to snatch your life. It dreams to choke you and wishes your *Li* to be death. There is a grimace in her dark face, yet gracefulness in her dance. All men pray they are never seduced by this sadistic raven."

"You are a spook, Koli," someone shouted.

Koli turned and snapped at the man, "In every man's heart exists some fear. Must you create more by suspecting this youth?"

"You love him too much," the one along the railing chastised.

"Even *you* fear death!"

"Those are Bintu words!" another shouted, leaping towards Koli.

"Ha! Ha!" Biano laughed, stopping the attacker's advance. A gruff, deliberate voice roared out across the deck and broke all sound.

"You laugh, but Topet was my brother!"

And before Rolind could focus on the voice, strong hands lifted him by his loose shirt collar and the crotch of his pants. The youth coughed and gagged, gasping for air. His attacker shouted, "Speak or I'll split you in half!"

Another powerful hand landed across the assailant's gut, doubling him over and freeing his grip on Rolind.

The boy fell hard against the solid deck and landed by Biano's feet and for a moment visualized the black whipping belts and the silver blade.

"Leave him alone!"

Rolind recognized Mansano's coarse voice. "Murder will not revive your brother, Plio. Now back to work!" Then Mansano's powerful grip lifted Rolind up from the deck and as the others meekly stepped aside, he led the boy away. When they reached the captain's door, Rolind tried to break free, but the Kinu pushed him roughly through. Then the Kinu turned and left the boy to stand alone. As Lermo looked up, Rolind shouted out above his tears, "He is rude! There is no need for Mansano to be so rude!"

"Would you wish the others to suspect your identity and have him find you dead one morn?"

Rolind stared into Lermo's eyes, then away towards the tankard of rum resting in a circular groove cut in the dark oak desk. As the captain brought the liquid to his lips, he spoke in gentle tones.

"A murder occurred last night. And probably it is no more a secret among the crew, for Plio seeks revenge, and the others fear that even more death will come. There is rumor that you wandered late last night, yet none astir remembers you."

"I have no more need for murder. My own act was caused by trickery."

"There is no accusation, just inquisitiveness. I plan to snatch these ghouls."

"Why do Bintus sail your ship!" Rolind demanded, trying to divert the captain's thoughts.

"There are none left of those who sailed the Lidu craft, only those who murdered yesterday and they are converts: Merus, Gimbus, Kisus, Nidus . . . all devoid of *Lis*. They fear some creature called Kana, and grant him human lives for appeasement. If they would kill each other off I wouldn't bother to seek them out, but they convert from ordinary men who cry out with pain."

Rolind turned to face the saber on the wall. The tip flowed red with blood. After a moment of grim memories, he held back the swell of anguish and stared demandingly at the captain's eyes.

"Then you see me as a murderer for what my father planned for me!"

"No such thoughts flourish in my mind. But those who do not know your special case only hear your nightmares, and see your look of fear. To them you are a perfect convert to enter their ways."

Again the youth turned to face the saber. Tears began to flow.

"Do you feel an obligation to these men, seeing yourself as they are? Or is it that you fear their daggers?" Lermo demanded.

"I fear nothing," Rolind snapped back. "I fear nothing! Nothing! Nothing! Do you understand!?"

"Yet a dead man's dagger missed you on the quarterdeck and your face seemed fearful!"

Rolind drew his head upward and refused to speak. And if he could, he would have refused to hear.

"You have seen too much aboard this ship, Rolind. There is no safety among these men."

"No!" Rolind spoke through choking tears. "I have signed up as a member of this crew and the voyage isn't over yet!"

"You were invited aboard this ship for only *one* purpose," Lermo began.

But Rolind shouted out, "Clocks and candles! Candles and clocks! That is all which surrounds me!" recalling the crippled soothsayer's words. "Is there none who will listen to me!?" Then staring up, he shouted out, "You have no right to restrict my freedom! I am the King!"

"Aboard this ship, Rolind, I decide what rights exist. *Your* kingdom lies back in Meru; mine, aboard *these* decks."

Rolind resented the captain's words and walked defiantly toward the starboard window, staring out into the horizon of chopping waves. His voice came soft as images of Dels' crypt flashed before his eyes.

"My father also planned great moments for my life." Then he turned to face the man. "He, too, decided what was right. And by his plans caused me all this grief! Is not to die perhaps a better way to spend the time than enslaved by another's rule!"

Lermo rose and approached the sulking boy. His touch

upon Rolind's shoulders drew the boy's eyes up towards his.

"I cannot watch you die, Rolind. For this voyage *you* chose the treasure and I feel obligated to get you there. If you wish another route, quickly shall I aim this vessel there. But you are not a sailor and the dangers aboard the *Voyager* are greater than you know."

Rolind slid from under Lermo's hand and back towards the door, and stopping before it, found himself caught between the echoing demands his father had once placed upon his life, and this stranger's expression of concern. Suddenly the cabin door flew open, shattering all calm, and driving his heart to stop. The sunlight blinded his eyes. A sailor rushed past, shouting, "Captain! Captain! She flies off the starboard quarter! Pheasant in her galley and jewels upon the mast. Just a glance reveals silken sails. Ah, what a prize, my Captain. What a snatch. She is Kidu and fast approaches for attack!"

Lermo arose and ran, pushing the youth onto the poop deck and holding him there. The north wind blew hard, and overhead the sails flapped and bellowed full. The *Voyager* headed southwest; full sails appeared in the northeast. Lermo peered through a long black tube while the crew scurried up the three masts, positioning themselves along the yards, and others climbed out of hatches and cleared the deck of rope and sail. Within the mast-castles fires were lit and the pungent odor of boiling oil soon struck Rolind's nose. He looked up to watch men stirring the black syrupy liquid with long poles. Hot droplets splattered on the planks. The distant sails steadily approached and three men leaned heavy on the *Volager*'s long rudder handle. Lermo stoically peered through the long looking glass.

"These Lidus are insane," he said without looking up. "They aim to ram us, yet the wind blows equally for both ships. A collision would half our hull and split their bow. The sea is smooth enough for us to meet her port side and clash with swords. She's flying three lateens!"

Rolind rolled his hand before one eye, forming a shaft through which to view the oncoming vessel, seeing tall aft triangular sails slipping wind.

"Her captain must be a magician if he plans to board

and pillage us," Lermo continued. "Or else a fool expecting the *Voyager* to maintain a straight course and be rammed."

Rolind continued to watch the enlarging sails, no longer needing his hand-made shaft and looking up apprehensively.

Suddenly the captain bellowed out.

"Furl the mainsail and mizzen! Hard rudder, left!"

The words echoed across the deck by chiefs who commanded each mast. The yardsmen working feverishly, furling the large sails, and causing the ship to lurch as the quarter wind slipped through the newly formed space. Rolind fell down. The *Voyager* quickly charged the wind, and salt spray hit the youth as he rose to watch the attacking vessel, her mainsails appearing large enough to cast the *Voyager* into shadow, her yards boasting a line of men. Her deck was a glitter of swords and cutlasses. The solid tan keel cut the sea ahead, throwing white caps all around. And though the *Voyager* continued to turn, Rolind held his breath and closed his eyes, expecting a great explosion in the air.

But as his lungs begged for breath, Rolind opened his twitching eyelids in time to watch the sleek Lidu ship sail full-power by. Rolind looked up to catch sight of leather pouches, each about the size of a man, falling from the yardcastles, and landing upon the Lidu quarter-deck. Hot black oil splattered and danced along the sea-soaked wood, while screams of scalded men pierced his ears. Crew members of the *Voyager* screamed out a cheer and Rolind looked up to Lermo for an explanation of the appalling sight. But the captain ignored the boy's stare and maintained his stoic, vigilant command.

"Hard right rudder!"

In a moment the *Voyager* returned parallel to her original course.

"Catch wind!" and the wide rectangular sails dropped from the main and mizzenmasts. Lermo turned to face the bewildered youth.

"It's not over yet. Now she'll give us chase."

Rolind stared portside, watching the Lidu ship, her mainsails suddenly furled, and she began turning wide, directing her lateens directly towards the *Voyager*.

"Now she'll run on her lateens," Lermo explained. "The wind would drive hard against unfurled mainsails. But now the wind will pull her across the waves. She's a sleek vessel, and even against this wind, much faster than we."

Rolind turned to face a concerned voice.

"There will be swords and blood, Rolind. I shall lock you in my cabin."

Rolind looked up at the fast-approaching ship.

"No!" he suddenly roared. "I shall stay here! Death and I have met before. There is no more fear in me."

The two stared at each other. Finally Lermo handed Rolind his dagger. "Then carry this."

The boy cast the weapon away.

"No! I will strike no other man! I shall never kill again!"

"If you refuse, the men will surely call you traitor and seek revenge for your treachery against them. Each man aids all others in battle. But were you to hide they would think you hurt. There is no shame in that! Were you one of us, the rule would be different. And should you die . . . No, I would never permit that!"

Rolind turned away, watching the almost colliding Lidu ship. Lermo drew his sword.

"You are most immature, sire."

V

As the sails of the *Voyager* were quickly secured, men lined the decks with glistening blades. The Lidu ship fast approached her keel, then turned to lean against the *Voyager*'s port-side. The roar of a hundred sailors pierced the air. Ropes enjoined the two ships and hot oil danced upon the decks, beading across the wood and crackling a deadly song. The ships crashed waist to waist, and the sharp sound of cracking timbers mingled among the sounds of clashing steel and frenzied men. Blood poured from chests and a head rolled by Rolind's feet. He stood, frozen, watching the lifeless stare roll overboard. Suddenly a rude arm surrounded the boy and lifted him easily, casting him against the solid floor of Lermo's cabin. The door slammed shut, immersing the youth in darkness.

He angrily arose, preparing to set out again, but an image of the rolling head ceased his advance. Heavy boots pounded above his head and the sounds of clashing steel rang through the dark room. Suddenly he turned and faced the cutlass on the wall, approaching it, determined to hold the weapon in his grip. But as his hand reached out, he stood frozen, peering into images which pulsated from its ornate silver-ringed handle: Dels's long wreath of pain; the flagellations of black leather belts; a hysterical gaping mouth with broken teeth; a pointing finger, with accusations at its tip; echoing screams of death.

Back he stepped, unable to scream as tears rolled slowly down his cheeks.

A blunt tip struck his side and Rolind wheeled around, reaching out for the tankard of rum. Quickly he downed the drink. The sounds of battle consumed all sense. But quickly did the hot, buttery rum melt all sound and dried his tears away. A numbness struck the brain and a smile slowly crossed his face. As he stared behind closed eyes, Dels's face flashed again and Rolind screamed and threw the mug away. But the image faded fast and upon his knees he fell, reaching out behind a sudden flood of tears to find more rum and drown the fear.

Whimpering became his voice and hysterical laughter filled his brain. The boy arose, toppling at first; but he finally stood erect. Then staggering towards the cutlass on the wall, held the weapon en guarde, facing an image of his father at the door. And he aimed the blade to pierce the chest, and cut the beating heart in half. He charged with all the fury of his hate, and rammed every bit of his strength into the form, crying out, demanding that it die! die! die!

But when the figure remained before his eyes, Rolind laughed, then cried, then laughed again. Soon his sight was washed away by tears, and laughter numbed his thoughts and his weeping body fell unconscious to the floor.

VI

As the youth awoke he felt the softness of a bed and the penetration of a gentle stare. Lermo sat in repose beside him and Rolind momentarily reached out to touch the form, but suddenly withdrew into a senseless void. His head fell weakly as he faced the sunlit windows above him. No vision flowed within.

"I find it necessary to confine you to my quarters, Rolind. The scene without would cause too much terror for your mind."

"No," Rolind weakly protested. "I need my freedom to feel at ease."

"You suffer most nobly, sire, but thus far it pains me to know your case. Perhaps it would be wiser to return you to Meru and the sanctuary of your domicile."

"NO! NO! NO! You can't." Suddenly appalled by the stain of blood across a freshly mutilated flap of skin, he fell limply back again.

"Already you have seen too much aboard this ship, and still the danger grows. Bintus freely walk the decks."

"It's all your fault," Rolind whimpered, seeing his father's face before his own. Then Lermo's scar reappeared.

"There is no cause for disagreement," the captain said. "But only you can reveal who these Bintu are. Only then can we be rid of them."

"No! No! I wish no part of this!" Rolind looked anxiously at the door, then up to the wall where the saber sat. "Is it not enough to have once been a tool of murder? Do you force me to further participation in the sport?"

"Sport?" the captain shouted with surprise. "You speak nonsense, sire."

"Nonsense?" Rolind cried out. "Is it nonsense to refuse the cause of pain?"

"But by your silence death will surely come. Another human sacrifice, and then another. Soon other weak men will join their cult and more will die. These creatures are a cancer, sire. Let them thrive and soon their vileness will infest both you and me. I admit the truth that many Bintu sail the sea aboard Meru ships, and by their infection the empire daily weakens. But your silence only aids them to destroy our peaceful home."

"Peaceful home!" Rolind sat up. "How can you speak of peace when continuously I find myself immersed in plots of death? Of what peaceful kingdom do you speak? Only one of pain has been revealed to me."

"Then surely your world is far divorced from ours," the captain gently said. "Within the confines of this realm others find their peace. It is our manner, lest some foreign mind conceives great violence for our lives. Truly Merus seek no other way. Has some great enemy burdened your life with suffering?"

Rolind turned away. A shadowed stain of blood spoiled the wall before him.

"Perhaps the Meru aboard this ship are gruff," the captain continued, "but in none exists any wishes for death. But danger demands violence in defense."

"Only violence and fear do I recall within my fifteen years. That is why I search the flower of the storm. In it lies the promise of eternal and personal peace. One very wise has told me this."

"Then we shall find it, sire, but only if we live to man the course."

Rolind hesitated, falling into deep reflection, seeing the magic red petals dance before his eyes. The song which Tiki had sung that day echoed in his mind:

And upon this soil the seed shall spring
and flowers blossom full
and into all men's lives shall come
the peaceful kingdom's rule.

These things I sing to you
speak of present dreams

but also of a latter-day
filled with happy scenes.

For though our sorrow sings today
and echoes through our land
the sun shall always warm again
the coldest, oldest man.

He dropped his legs over the bed and exposed the gash along his calf, holding it high for the captain's eyes.

"This," he slowly ran a finger along the wound, "is how you know their names."

Lermo stood transfixed by the wound. Then after staring into Rolind's distant gaze he rose to face the door.

"One request, Captain," Rolind humbly called out, stopping Lermo's advance. "Call me to Kaiso to give me a word of comfort, and bring me Tiki to sing a song of cheer."

Lermo quietly turned and, after blankly staring into Rolind's eyes, approached the bowed head.

"To bring Tiki would cause no pain, but Kaiso lies among the slain."

"No!" Rolind screamed, biting the skin over his wrist. "No! It cannot be! It makes no sense to me that one so mild should die and I so filled with guilt should live!"

The young king drew back across the bed with fear, turning back to face images of peace which had flourished in his brain. Lermo grabbed the youth and, holding him dear, forced Rolind to cry against his chest.

"Sometimes I feel as though there is someone deep inside," Rolind moaned, "scratching at my eyes, fighting to get outside! But how do I let him out!"

Lermo gently held the crying boy away and, staring deeply into his eyes, declared, "Let me tell you how it is, sire. We speed at ten knots to that stormy spot. By evening shall we rest and, with the aid of stars above know if it be the storm we find."

Rolind quieted at the captain's words.

"Beyond us lies the Kidu ship in flames, aboard us lies the stains of blood once men. I fear for you. The storm may bring you nothing more than pain."

"Then surely I have nothing more to fear," Rolind

said. With a gentle finger he surveyed Lermo's fresh wound. Then he turned away to stare into the dark brown wood, his mind devoid of words. Suddenly he called out from deep within his fear, "And these Bintu, Lermo, you will hang them from the yards?"

"No, sire, not like that. Too much death has already passed your eyes. I couldn't burden you with more."

"But I will know, regardless of the way."

Lermo rose and stepping away spoke cautiously to the youth. "When we reach the spot, I shall call your name. 'Tis best you rest away this day. I shall have Mansano bring food and, in good time, the physician to dress your wound."

Rolind reached down to touch the gash, then shut his eyes, trying to block out all memories. And as Lermo left the room he leaned back into sensations of deepest fear. Then cast upon a cloud of tears, he fell into a troubled, tortured sleep.

A violent jerk awoke the youth and made him face the darkness of the room. As he turned to search the space, he caught a glimpse of Lermo lighting an oil lamp. The room began to glow. The entire cabin swayed. As Rolind got up he could feel great swells smash against the hull, and he struggled to remain upright. Lermo beckoned him to come. And though fearful that a universe of juries stood beyond the door, Rolind meekly walked, out into the storm.

When upon the deck he searched around for evidence of death, yet all he saw were men who carried buckets to the rails and others slung across the yards securing sails. Lermo stopped him on the center deck. Walls of salt spray slapped his face and as the storm raged Rolind struggled out to see. But no peaceful island stood beyond the clouds.

"It is night, sire. Yet were it day such difficulty would exist in finding an easy place to stand. Grab anything!" the Captain shouted as Rolind nearly fell upon his knees. The hardy voice became muffled beneath the power of the wind.

Rolind held onto a mainsail line and stared. Never in his life had he seen such a wall of thick, black clouds. He searched for light. A sudden clap of thunder made him jump.

"Have no fear," Lermo shouted out. "The thunder comes from within the center of the storm. It is only wind we feel. Yet these fierce waves will easily splinter our waist should we wait too long."

"And the sage?" Rolind's voice creaked out.

"Perhaps he too did flee this spot, for, by the stars, we ride exactly where last we made rendezvous just eight days ago."

"But he had the flower and knows the place!" Rolind shouted out. "Why should he abandon it?"

Lermo remained still and Rolind quickly returned to staring into the blackness before him. Rain soaked his hair as he turned portside in hope the old man's raft would appear.

"Perhaps we could wait for his return," Rolind begged, looking up to his companion for confidence. But Lermo remained mute, and the youth stared back into the storm. Then his frustration grew and he shouted out, "Then let us search the sea! We cannot wait forever!"

The Captain turned to face the outraged voice, but his manner was most straightforward and calm. "We dare not proceed much further beyond this spot, sire. To explore uncharted seas with such a fragile craft as this would be as foolish as seeking death. We shall wait, but not too long. Our planks weaken with each strike of the sea, and the men are fatigued from pumping water from our hold.

Rolind looked up, angered, but with restrained voice, his eyes catching sight of the oarsboat which had first carried him to the *Voyager*. Lermo turned toward his cabin and spoke.

"You must come back within. It will be drier for us there."

"No, Lermo," Rolind begged, his sight steady toward the craft. "Just this while I wish to stare into the sea and contemplate all I know and all which has just occurred to me."

His words came slowly and Lermo hesitated for a while.

But Rolind settled blankly on the rail, and Lermo left him unattended in the storm.

With Lermo out of sight, Rolind cautiously approached the starboard side, staring out across the thrashing sea. Securely holding onto coarse, wet rope he was tossed violently by the waves. Echoes of the soothsayer's words, were secure within his mind: *And in this land stand three earthen mounds . . .*

"I shall be able to spot them" he fantasized. "After all, they must be unique and large."

. . . shall come the peaceful kingdom's rule. Rolind's mind recalled the words *. . . shall come the peaceful kingdom's rule.*

"Perhaps it had all been conceived," he thought. "A scheme, a lie, words to satiate my thoughts or perhaps to make me celebrate *this life.*"

Then into his ear a scream of Dels's recurring death blared out. Rolind stared deeply through the crystal line of white-caps and the scream dissolved.

"Of course it's there," he cried.

"Now!" he shouted into the storm. "I've got to find it now!" And spotting none other by the oarsboat he ran quickly there. Once upon the spot, he grabbed the pulley-rope and pulled hard enough to crank the small vessel over the rail and down below the surface of the deck. Then, jumping into its shell, he manipulated the ropes from within. By releasing the winch-lines and pushing against the girdle of the merchant ship, Rolind found himself quickly floundering free upon the sea.

Oh, how he fought the waves with heavy oars, finding himself quickly swallowed by the bleakness of the storm, and heading straight for the darkest spot before his eye; for there he pictured mountains gathering clouds and beyond that stormy wall the magic island, bright with sun. And though he had set straight off for exploration without concern, there came the anguished burst of painful pasts. Yet he drove on amidst the tears, hearing concerts of the crippled soothsayer's words, imagining a peacefulness beyond the storm, the joy he hoped could come of it. Oh, how wonderful, to claim the magic flower singularly as his alone.

Tears mixed with salty spray, the steady downpour washing them away. He felt the sea's crash against the tiny craft and the whistling brutal wind pierce his ears, renewing sounds of pain and the sounds of steel clashing. A dismembered head rolled by his eye and blood-colored waves foamed death. And he floated, crippled in his mind, floundering on the torrid waves, unable to guide the small, fragile craft.

He arose with impassioned screams, then fell back against the folded sail, whimpering feverishly, an injured pup, wiping dry his face, ridding from his mind the scenes, but finding new ones emerge with every tear.

Then an impact lurched the ship, knocking Rolind aft and across the wooden seats. The sound of cracking timber made him spin around.

Red faces; eyes; hands reaching out to grab, jumping as though from the very portion of the storm, driving this boy back with fear, grappling at his arms and head, dragging him away.

Hysterically he screamed, demanding them away, blindly striking back with limp arms, then wishing for some death to end his mind now red with rage. He screams out words, then whimpers meekly on his back. Then up again to blindly battle sensations he cannot feel . . .

. . . the night, then light; concentric rings flash, then reverberate . . .

. . . a frost; and then warmth . . . a cry; a reaching out to see . . .

. . . and then, at last, to sleep.

vii

LERMO GUIDED THE CATATONIC YOUTH from the wooden docks and along the flat-stone streets, past merchant ships and the clap of wagons against the rocks. But the sights all passed as blurs, and the sounds as distant thuds. Unusually quiet was Rolind's mind.

And limply did he drag his feet, as a puppet would, to scale the granite steps which spiraled from the streets below to where the castle stood. Lermo led him step-by-step past the gardens bright with golden poppies and glowing swirls of orange puffballs. The fountains gurgled blue and irridescent fish filled the ponds while seagulls soared above. But all this passed the boy-king's distant stare.

And through the portcullis did they walk unhindered by the stoic guards, to stand within the hall of mirrors, before which Rolind stopped to peer. Wordlessly did he twirl about to find a hundred mindless sets of eyes all staring out. He drew a heavy breath, then dropped his head and stopped. Lermo turned the youthful figure round and led him out.

Then they crossed the lengths of corridors, immersed in echoes of their steps, and ascended marble stairs up to the public chamber. A solemn Tyre met them there.

"Sire." The mentor reached out and held the sightless youth against his chest.

Lermo bowed his head, then turned, and slump-shouldered, walked away. The echo died and Tyre kissed the young king's head. Without a word he led the youth up to the solitary throne, and set him there. With ease he placed the crown upon his head.

"You are home." Tyre placed the golden locket around Rolind's neck.

The youth looked up blankly towards the mentor's face. He saw a frown appear and reached out to wipe it away. But a solemn voice drove his finger back.

"Sire, whilst you were away, many evils did pass."

Rolind faced his mentor's eyes.

"One night Plio stumbled upon Vernon who donned the golden crown of Byiu kings, and while he slew him in a rage, Caji surprised the two. Great battles raged within the chamber walls."

Rolind sat up, suddenly more conscious, yet unsure of what he heard. Tyre's voice held him captive to the words.

"Then Jani entered and rammed his sword through Caji's back, then with a scythe mutilated Vernon's corpse as Stel, your councillor from the Kinu tribes, stole Jani's life and as the Meru elders—still guests in the castle, and one of them your uncle, Sila—happened upon the scene; the castle flowed with a bath of blood."

Rolind looked up aghast, afraid to move, his mind, devoid of comprehension, pleading behind blinded eye for Tyre to cease his speech.

"Your mother, seeing much blood on the floor, fled to the eastern village, Ruon."

Rolind rose to flee.

"The throne is stained with blood."

Quickly did he back away. The touch of cold wood made him lift his hand away.

"Their bones all rest within the gardens by the inner wall."

"No!" Rolind screamed violently shaking his head, dropping down the crown and tearing away the locket, trying to cast away the images which flowed within his brain. But the mentor's voice continued with more words of blood and Rolind blindly shook his head. Suddenly he turned and fled down the corriders so well known to him.

"No!" he screamed as though about to dispel all pain.

He swung wide the secret boulder, the only exit which he knew. Tears streamed down to wash his cheeks.

Down the length of the hill he ran, blindly past his favorite Joshua trees, and across the cobblestones, his screams muffling the slap of his bare feet.

Amidst his blinded rage there came horses that he

failed to see, six hearty steeds with clamering bells, their powerful hooves lifting high to drop his frenzied form against the hard rock surface of the road. Rolind screamed until the solid, massive-weighted cart of sassal ropes split his torso in cataclysmic pain beyond all consciousness, and drove him lifeless into death!

Old women, imps, the passing crowd hurried to the scene, tugging at his undefinable form, aghast at images of their own inevitable demise. And even while the strangers gawked and stepped back in fear, no peace could Rolind find, for the flies began at once, molesting, pecking at his freshly mutilated skin.

The sun beat down and quickly did he rot.

VI

i

THE ROYAL CASTLE OF MERU stood bleached beneath a late noon sun. All seemed lifeless within, save a soft-spoken voice speaking out from the obiel of Rolind's room.

"Do you see those peaks in the distant south?" A long wrinkled finger pointed out beyond the tall rectangular frames. "There lies the boundary of this kingdom which now we rule. And there," it drew a line across the palisade to a southern, distant shore, "lies the kingdom which the Lidu rule. And in the west, the Asu. But fortunate are we to control this land of Meru, for its commerce alone creates the strength of those other realms."

"And we shall serve the cause," responded a dark-haired fifteen-year-old whose features to the unobservant eye would make one swear he must be Rolind—truly king of Meru and most assuredly alive.

Tyre drew the youth closer to his knee and, as he turned him round, placed a kiss upon his cheek. As the boy looked up, the mentor placed the ancient Byiu crest across his chest.

"You shall make a fine king, my Bintu son, for I see Rolind in your eyes."

"And this Rolind, where dwells he now?"

"Somewhere down below." Tyre pointed to the twisting streets. "Rolind runs mad with rage, blind with fear. And before the evening ends, shall he be sacrificed to face Kana. For surely did Rolind suffer such great pain as to become the Kana's equal."

"Your love for him must have been as great as any man can conceive."

Tyre smiled, nodding approval of this youth's choice of words. "For fifteen years did I raise him as my son. And because of love did he suffer as he did. Not a drop of malice ever stained my heart. Now it shall be *you* who will wear his crown."

"And the throne, how did you secure it?"

"By carefully drawn plan. For five Meru reigns have Bintu teachers served the young pretenders to the throne. The recommendation of one, thought to be a Sessu, insured our role. Long did we wait for some unsuspected act to aid the cause, perhaps to find some princely substitute from among our Bintu youth. But no easy matter would it be. For simply to kill the king would raise suspicion of a Bintu plot and perhaps create a war. And then the twins were born. Never had there been more than one pretender to the throne, for always when a prince was born, did they insure the queen would no more conceive. It has always been a Meru fear that the history of Awio would again repeat itself and create destructive competition for the throne. It was an easy thing to convince King Riis that only a princely duel would resolve the obvious conflict at hand."

"And did not the twins seek a solution of their own?"

"Of course. While Dels would merely read away the hours, Rolind sought some grand escape. Yet never did he move without a spy around; from the Joshua cluster where he hid his clothes, to the cornfields where he feigned a personality diverse and free from woe. If he had not chosen to return here for the duel, some trick of ours would have brought him back. But when, in front of his father's court he proclaimed some evidence to dispel the need to battle Dels, did I search his room and stole the book. When Riis came to seek it out, I convinced the man that Rolind often muttered deliriously about a diary which cast the Book of Orange in doubt. And of course they dueled."

"And what if Dels had won the fight?"

"Then, perhaps, my Bintu son, you would not be king, for Dels truly was the stronger of the two and would have accepted his brother's death as fate. But I had no worry, for not only did each prince receive an aggressive drug, but Dels received one other to effect his sight."

"Truly a masterful game of *Jackal,* superbly won." The slender-cheeked youth turned to face the distant mountains of his native land. "And shall the seige begin this month?"

"Oh, no. Just as careful planning and patience destroyed the recent line of Meru kings, must our victory be assuredly won. The proof of this kingdom's strength was felt when another Lidu-seized ship failed to destroy Lermo's crew and kill the youth at sea. Great unity from fear unites the fifteen tribes, and in a war many Bintu men would die. And there's no reason any man should die, when for all his days alive he can suffer pain. But," Tyre assured the boy with a gentle grip, "with you as king, we can plant suspicion of the Alsu with the Sessu, the Gimbu of the Nesu, just as we incited Callio and his troops of Kinu to attack the Meru tribe. And when they fiercely quarrel and their allegiances diverge, the Bintu troops shall cross the mountainous terrain without a fight. Already we have men throughout every town and ship to implement such subversive plans. And yet it might not be we who live to see it through. But nevertheless it will come. After all, what greater purpose do we have in life than to insure all men a strength against the Kana?"

The mentor's eyes watered as he thought of victory and feverishly he rose to survey the conquered realm. As he spoke, visions flowed.

"We shall castrate all their males and force their women to bear a race prepared to tolerate the Kana's wrath." Then turning to the youth, he proudly said, "Come, my son. Certainly you make a splendid king. Let us be prepared." He led the newly crowned ruler beyond the door. "The tribal elders will gather in five days' time to chose new councillors for your aid, and there are royal manners which you must learn."

Then he spoke with pride, fully conscious of the scars upon his legs. "The moon shall rise full tonight, and we, together, shall reveal to Kana how great is our strength."

ODE TO ROLIND

What are you child

if not a creature of games, donning uniforms and disguises
seeking out the complexity of life
searching out a peace within the universe
and contentment with your mind?

What are you child

if not the lessons of your trials
if not the dreams which stimulate your mind
if not a personality begging expression in a reality so undefined
if not one tiny speck amongst the countless elements within the universe
if not a creature crying out in desperation, begging me who cannot read your thoughts or sense your fears to understand?

Does it take each generation of man

the murder of his kin
to make him understand
every man's relationship to him?

Or shall there be a way

to plant this lesson in the grave
and blossom for our children
a flower for their day, a flower
that will radiate the song,
to teach the way?

Are these obdurations in the night

which create the consciousness and light
to awaken mankind from the plight
of nature's wary flight

from those decades
when the human was a creature in the mud
and such a need
meant survival of the seed?

And shall there ever come a day

when the pain of life shall wane
and with our consciousness ablaze
understand that life is just a game devoid of rules?

But if it be the plan

to keep your nature as a man
won't you turn and face the grave
and rally with the knowledge
that one day
your suffering shall fly amongst the particles of time.

Who are you child

if not the jewel of my eye
if not the questioning of mind
if not the answer to my universal, why?

if not my search throughout eternal time,
who I reach out to with this peace of mine?

And what be I

if not a child

once upon a time?

AVON MEANS THE BEST IN FANTASY AND SCIENCE FICTION

URSULA K. LE GUIN

The Lathe of Heaven	25338	1.25
The Dispossessed	24885	1.75

ISAAC ASIMOV

Foundation	29579	1.50
Foundation and Empire	30627	1.50
Second Foundation	29280	1.50
The Foundation Trilogy (Large Format)	26930	4.95

ROGER ZELAZNY

Doorways in the Sand	32086	1.50
Creatures of Light and Darkness	27821	1.25
Lord of Light	33985	1.75
The Doors of His Face, The Lamps of His Mouth	18846	1.25
The Guns of Avalon	31112	1.50
Nine Princes in Amber	27664	1.25
Sign of the Unicorn	30973	1.50
The Hand of Oberon	33324	1.50

Include 25¢ per copy for postage and handling,
allow 4-6 weeks for delivery.

Avon Books, Mail Order Dept.
250 W. 55th St., N.Y., N.Y. 10019

SF 6-77

NEW LEADER IN SCIENCE FICTION

672 pages 34009 $2.25

Edited by
Robert Silverberg

The greatest science fiction short stories of all time chosen by the Science Fiction Writers of America.

"DEFINITIVE!"
Lester del Rey

VOLUME I

"A BASIC ONE-VOLUME LIBRARY OF THE SHORT SCIENCE FICTION STORY."
Algis Budrys

HFVI 5-77

FOR THE FIRST TIME IN PAPERBACK, FOUR SPACED-OUT FANTASIES OF CHILLING SATIRE AND MIND-BENDING FUTURISM FROM THE MODERN MASTER OF SCIENCE FICTION:

THE CYBERIAD 27201 $1.50
The intergalactic capers of two "cosmic constructors" as they vie to out-invent each other building gargantuan cybernetic monsters all across the universe.

THE FUTUROLOGICAL CONGRESS 28720 $1.25
A traveler from outer space comes to Earth for a conference, but a revolution catapults him into a synthetic future paradise created by hallucinogenic drugs.

THE INVESTIGATION 29314 $1.50
When dead bodies inexplicably resurrect themselves, a shrewd detective and an adroit statistician match metaphysical wits in a case that lies beyond mind, beyond this world.

MEMOIRS FOUND IN A BATHTUB 29959 $1.50
Far in the future, a man wanders pointlessly in the designed destiny of a vast underground labyrinth, the final stronghold of the American Pentagon.

"A major figure who just happens to be a science fiction writer . . . very likely, he is also the bestselling SF writer in the world."
Fantasy and Science Fiction

LEM 8-76